# The Ivy Plot

# The Ivy Plot

**Dayle Courtney**

Illustrated by
**John Ham**

STANDARD PUBLISHING
Cincinnati, Ohio                                    2714

## *Thorne Twins* Adventure Books

Library of Congress Cataloging in Publication Data

Courtney, Dayle.
   The Ivy plot.

   (Thorne Twins adventure books ; 4)
   Summary: When sixteen-year-olds Eric and Alison dis-
cover a secret Nazi organization in their hometown, Eric,
with his Christian values, decides to infiltrate.
   [1. Fascism—Fiction. 2. Christian life—Fiction. 3. Twins
—Fiction] I. Ham, John. II. Title. III. Series: Courtney,
Dayle. Thorne Twins adventure books ; 4.
PZ7.C83158Iv            [Fic]                    81-5631
ISBN 0-87239-469-7                              AACR2

Copyright © 1981, The STANDARD PUBLISHING Company, Cincinnati, Ohio.
A division of STANDEX INTERNATIONAL Corporation. Printed in U.S.A.

# Contents

# 1 • *Dangerous Investigation*

A dark, huddled mass slowly detached itself from the shadows, drew erect, and loped across the moonlit grass. Before dissolving into the onrushing landscape, its fleeting profile disclosed the features of a young man—features disfigured by fear.

He ran erratically in a wild, stumbling, headlong course, darting furtive glances over his shoulder.

*Catch a nigger by the toe*
*If he hollers—*

The taunting, degrading words swept over Paul Earl as the events of that evening crystallized in his mind.

At least his black skin would provide cover in the enveloping night, he thought bitterly.

His mind kept turning the words over and over. Round and round they spun in his frightened mind. But at the center of his thoughts was one recurring fear rising slowly now: The sheriff was out to kill him, no two ways about it. Dead men tell no tales.

7

Far away, a sharp clear sound broke out of the surrounding stillness. It built to a volley of loud, raucous yaps of unleashed eagerness and furious devotion to the hunt. The sheriff's killer pack of wolfhounds—a vicious breed of manhunters.

Paul knew an instant of freezing terror. His heart thudding painfully in his throat, he fled, crashing through the bushes. He felt naked and helpless.

He darted through the dark pine trees sighing in the wind of night. Their branches met overhead in a continuous tangle, screening the stars. There were brambles to dodge, low boughs to dive under. Clinging vines clutched at his trousers. The tangled undergrowth thickened.

A sudden convulsion of rage shook him. He was being pursued by Nazis!

It had all begun with a tip called into the Midwest University newspaper about a secret Nazi organization called Phoenix. In the news office at the time, reporter Paul Earl answered the phone.

The tip had been anonymous, but a lead worth following up, Paul thought. The caller had mentioned a pool hall at which some distinguished members of the Phoenix organization hung out in the town of Millbrook, six miles east of the Midwest University campus in Ivy.

Paul had asked the caller why he didn't report this Nazi activity to a daily newspaper. Why pick a college paper? The caller replied that a University professor was implicated, but he wouldn't elaborate. He was nervous, and hung up before Paul could draw him out.

Paul Earl biked the six miles over to Millbrook on a clear, sunlit day. His idea was to snoop around town,

8

sniffing out any information that might come to light. But if he had any hope of being inconspicuous, it was dashed as soon as he located the pool hall.

It occupied the upper level of a square two-story brick building. Paul sauntered in casually, and immediately sensed trouble. Three men dressed in government-issue khaki jackets swiveled around appraisingly. They were wearing brown armbands, but the significance escaped Paul at the time. Their momentary surprise gave way to a look of hard, concentrated menace.

One of them called over to him. He was a tall, droopy fellow with a mean, weasel-like face. "Hey, boy, didn't you see that sign outside? Minors not admitted. You don't claim to be a man, do you?"

Paul had a sudden sense of unreality, or of fantasy become reality. He must have heard those stock lines in old TV movies. Was he expected to take them seriously? But there was nothing unreal about these three goons, he reminded himself; they merely had Grade-B mentalities.

They were waiting for an answer, leering expectantly. What did the script call for? Paul's caution was swept aside in a sudden upswelling flood of hatred—hatred of the white boogeyman whose shadow had stalked his nightmares since he was a child.

"I've as much right to be here as you," he spat out.

The three started toward him. One of them had a chain!

Paul was reaching for an empty beer bottle, any prop to hold them off, when his arm was seized in midair. He struggled free.

"Simmer down, I'm the deputy sheriff." A trim,

firmly-knit man of about thirty studied him with a distinctly unfriendly air. "You have a right to be here, but don't press it." He motioned to the door.

Paul gagged on his indignation, but good sense prevailed. This isn't the time or place to make a stand, he told himself, and walked heavily down the stairs, the deputy following close behind.

As he rode off on his bike, he heard the three men complain, "Why didn't you let us fix him, Les?"

The answer was lost in traffic noise.

The whole trip was a zero, Paul thought disgustedly. Some reporter he was! Then he suddenly recalled the brown armbands. Didn't the Nazis wear those things?

He had gone a few miles or so down the road when he heard the wail of a police siren moving up fast behind him. It had nothing to do with him, but he pulled over to the side of the road, waiting for the patrol car to pass. To his surprise, it stopped beside him.

The sheriff and his deputy stepped out. Sheriff Dolan was a middle-aged man whose once athletic build was fast turning to fat. He had a habit of hitching up his trousers to contain his overflowing midsection.

"Do you have a license to drive that vehicle?" The sheriff's voice ripped the air like a power saw slicing a plant.

"The bike's not motorized. It doesn't need a license."

"You don't say? Is it registered?"

"No."

"Well now, you slipped up there, fella. Riding an unregistered bicycle is subject to a fine in Millbrook."

"All right, how much do I owe you?"

"Not so fast. Show me some ID."

Paul produced his wallet. The sheriff took it.

"Hmm, so you're a student at Midwest University. If this is your wallet."

"There's a photo on my student ID."

"Well now, I wouldn't swear it's you," said the sheriff, scratching his face. "All blacks photograph pretty much alike."

"You can confirm my identity with the University. Give them a call."

"This says your major is journalism. Work on the student paper?"

"Yes."

"What are you doing in Millbrook?"

"I'm here on personal business."

"Personal, huh? That's unusual, seeing there ain't but a smattering of blacks in Millbrook."

Paul remained silent.

"In my opinion, he's an outside agitator," the deputy said.

"That true, boy?" the sheriff asked.

"No," Paul said.

"I think Les is right. We can smell you agitators a mile off."

"Maybe I need a new underarm deodorant," Paul said.

The sheriff examined the rear of Paul's bike. "This taillight work?" he asked.

It didn't.

The sheriff scribbled in his notebook. He read it aloud: "Driving an unregistered vehicle without proper lighting, creating a public hazard. We're taking you in, boy."

"You're arresting me? For that? Look, sheriff, give me a ticket. I'm just passing through town."

"Don't tell me my job, boy. I'm booking you pending trial tomorrow."

"I've a right to one phone call," Paul shouted.

"Lower your voice," the sheriff growled. "You'll get your phone call—providing the phone's in order."

It wasn't.

It was the first time Paul had ever been behind bars. The cell was an airless, windowless room rank with the smell of disinfectant. He had a neighbor in the adjoining cell—the town drunk, rambling incoherently. Occasionally Paul picked out the word "Phoenix," but the drunk's speech was too slurred to be sure. Now and again he mumbled something about a "hunt." After a while, Paul gave up trying to understand.

Around six o'clock, the deputy, Les, brought Paul a tray of food—a ham sandwich, coffee, and pie.

"We don't want you to get weak," Les said, with a chuckle.

There was an unmistakable suggestion in his voice, a nuance of barely contained anticipation that Paul was unable to interpret. It made him even more uneasy.

After a short while, the sheriff and his deputy left the jail, slamming the door behind them. The jolt shook the door of Paul's cell. Paul watched it slide slowly open. Had Les deliberately left the door unlocked, hoping that Paul would attempt to escape?

Paul heard the police car roar off down the road, siren blaring.

*He might have forgotten to lock it,* Paul thought. But even if he could escape, it would be a stupid move.

His name and address were on record. On the other hand, he was sure to get a stiff fine, and since he wasn't carrying enough money to cover it, he'd be held over in jail for an indefinite period, cut off from the outside world. If he could make it back to Ivy, a smart lawyer would punch holes in the sheriff's case and sue the town for depriving his client of his constitutional rights.

The thought of spending another day in jail was intolerable. Let's say the escape was rigged. Maybe he could still make it. He was young and fast. Was it worth the gamble?

Paul pushed open the cell door and darted to a window. The street was empty. He glanced back at his cell, undecided. The drunk was cowering against the wall with a look of terror. "The hunt—" the man stammered. "The dogs—" For a moment he looked fully sober, struggling to frame a thought.

What hunt? Did the sheriff make a regular sport of chasing prisoners with dogs?

"Is the sheriff laying for me?" Paul asked. But the drunk was out cold again.

Paul searched the sheriff's desk for his wallet. There were a dozen wallets, his on top. How come the sheriff had never returned the other wallets? Could their owners all be dead?

The sky was beginning to darken. With sudden resolution, Paul ran to the back of the jail, pushed open a window, and—

He plunged among the bushes, tumbling over roots. His throat was dry, and sweat stood out in great beads on his face. From a distance he could hear the dogs barking, gaining on him. A cold tremor ran down his back.

He had covered about four miles of the distance back to Ivy. If he kept due west, he would emerge a half mile from the campus. His friend, Eric Thorne, would take him in. Eric's father, a professor at the University, would be able to advise him.

Paul stumbled upon a narrow path straggling through the woods. It led him to a small vine-covered cottage. The door was padlocked and the windows were barred. Paul felt a lightning flash of disappointment.

He called out. There was no answer.

"Please, somebody, help me!"

In a blind frenzy of despair, he hammered and beat against the unyielding door. He wasn't thinking straight. He had to keep moving. How many other escaped prisoners had come this way? He looked along the winding path that melted away into the distance, and plodded on, his eyes bleakly determined.

He followed a swell of land that dipped to the vale of a clear, rippling stream. Paul fell on his knees and thrust his face into the icy water. After slaking his thirst, he plunged into the stream, wading up to his knees. The water should wash away his scent.

A sudden growling sound brought Paul's taut nerves to the snapping point. His eyes opened wide as he swiveled around to face the bank. One of the dogs raced with wild frenzy along the shore. Its saber-like fangs, keen and brilliant as knives, flashed in a hungry snarl.

A pang of violent fear struck through Paul. He dug down under the water and came up with a rock.

"Get back! Back!" he cried, heaving the rock at the dog's feet.

Baring its teeth in rage, the dog swung to confront him. Paul immediately started downstream. Deadly eyes gleaming, eighty pounds of fury catapulted itself forward on top of him. The force of the impact drove the wind from Paul as he tumbled backward, his head under water. There was a singing in his ears, and his head fogged for a moment before he surfaced.

The dog was turning over and over, caught in the undertow of a churning eddy near the bank. The water spun him against the opposite bank. His head gave a sickening crack. The dog whined and sank limply beneath the surface.

Paul regained his feet and swallowed against sudden nausea. At his back he heard the other dogs yapping along the bank. He hoped he'd shaken them.

Alternately wading and floating down the stream for about half an hour, Paul pulled himself ashore and plunged into the trees. The woods soon opened upon a clearing marked by cement pylons. The highway passed within a hundred feet of where he stood!

He raced forward with a cry of joy the distance to the highway. A beam of yellow light shot out, blinding him. It passed quickly out of sight as an open van rumbled past and stopped a short distance down the road. Paul raced desperately after it, his heart thumping painfully against his ribs. With buckling knees, he launched himself, in a final spasm of energy, onto the back of the van and lay half dazed, his chest heaving, as the van rolled on to Ivy.

# 2 • *Uninvited Guest*

One, two, three, four. One, two, three, four.

The steady beat of the metronome was a monotonous accompaniment to the Czerny piano exercises. Alison Thorne could almost hear her piano teacher's stern Danish accent with each click of the swinging arm.

One, two, three—

A noise at the front door interrupted her concentration. A heavy thud. Alison stopped playing, turned off the metronome, and inclined her head slightly, listening intently.

It was a scraping sound—like someone raking fingers across a smooth wood surface.

Was someone at the door? At this hour? Her watch showed ten-thirty. If it was a legitimate caller, why didn't he knock or ring the bell?

Was that a moan? Or just the whine of the night wind?

Alison's twin brother, Eric, had turned in early and

was sleeping soundly in his room upstairs at the end of the hall. The rest of the house was empty. Their father, Dr. Randall Thorne, was away on a three-week lecture tour in Europe for the International Agricultural Foundation. And Aunt Rose, their father's widowed sister—who had mothered them as long as they could remember—had gone up to Chicago for her annual three-day spring shopping spree. They had insisted that she should go, and that they would get along fine for those few days she would be away.

Alison hated to disturb Eric. He was such a grouch when roused from a sound sleep. And it was probably unnecessary. Perhaps a cat was prowling outside.

It wasn't her nature to be skittish about unusual sounds in the night. As a child, it was Eric whose colorful imagination embroidered commonplace events. Alison considered herself sensible and well-balanced. So she decided to go investigate on her own.

Approaching the front door, she saw the knob turn. Then she heard another thud, like something falling against it.

Parting the window curtains at one side of the door, she saw a body doubled over, its weight pressing against the door.

"Who is it?" she murmured, her voice a breathless whisper.

There was no answer.

"Who—" she called, her voice catching in her throat.

This time she heard a shuddering moan.

Turning quickly, she raced up the stairs, propelling herself headlong into Eric's room.

"Wake up!" she shouted.

Eric sat bolt upright, eyes glazed with sleep. "Huh? What time is it?"

"Ten-thirty."

"Ten-thirty! What's the matter?"

"There's a body downstairs."

"A dead body?"

"I don't think so, not exactly."

"Alison, you must have had a bad dream. Go back to sleep." He gave a yawn and threw the blanket over his head.

Alison shook him by the shoulders. "I'm not dreaming. I haven't even gone to bed yet."

"That explains it. Keeping late hours. Burning the midnight oil. You're beginning to see things from nervous fatigue."

"Eric, get out of bed and come downstairs this instant. Someone is dying on the front porch, and all you think of is sleep!"

"You serious?"

Alison tugged at his arm.

"Oh, all right," he sighed. "Let me pull on my jeans."

Eric yawned and shuffled down the stairs, followed by Alison.

"You know what will happen, don't you?" Eric said. "By the time we get there, the body will be gone. Like in those kid's TV serials. And Homicide won't believe us. No *corpus delicti,* no murder."

As Eric glanced out the front window, he rocked back on his heels. "There really is a body."

"What do you think I've been telling you?"

He unlocked the door and swung it open. A man's

18

form lay sprawled across the threshold, face down. His clothes were wet, mud-spattered, and torn. Eric gently turned him over.

"Paul Earl!" The name exploded simultaneously from Eric's and Alison's lips.

"What happened to you?" Eric exclaimed.

Paul's mouth formed words, but his voice was a mere thread of sound.

"Help me get him inside," Eric said.

They grabbed him under the shoulders and pulled him through the doorway.

"I'll call an ambulance," Alison said.

"No," Paul murmured. "Water—please."

Alison dashed into the kitchen and returned with a glass of cool water. She wiped Paul's face with a damp hand towel, then raised the glass to his lips.

"Thanks," Paul whispered. "Sorry for the trouble. Just out on my feet, that's all."

"No trouble," Eric said. "You feel a little better?"

Paul nodded.

"Let's get him into a chair," Eric said.

Supporting him under the shoulders, they stood him erect on shaky legs and deposited him into an easy chair.

After Paul had rested a few minutes, Eric asked, "Do you feel up to telling us what happened?"

Paul sucked in his breath and, in a halting voice, recounted his experience in Millbrook.

"That's a bad scene," Eric said.

Alison brought in some milk and cookies. As Paul ate, she said, "I wonder where the sheriff fits into a Nazi scheme."

20

"I don't know," Paul said, his voice gaining strength. "Beyond the fact that he's a bigot and small-town tyrant—and, from all evidence, a *killer*. I didn't learn anything about Phoenix, that Nazi organization I went to check out."

"Millbrook may not even be the headquarters," Eric said, thinking out loud. "Just a place where some of the members hang out."

"That's possible," Paul said. "But then I didn't get a chance to see much of the town."

"Well, buddy," Eric said, "tonight you're parking here. Dad's away, and you can use his room."

"I'd better leave," Paul said, attempting to rise. His knees sagged, and he fell back into the chair.

"Yeah, sure, you're in great shape to leave," Eric said. "We'll see how you feel in the morning after a good night's rest."

Holding him around the waist, Eric and Alison helped him up the stairs to the bathroom. Paul washed, then wearing a pair of Eric's pajamas, he stretched out gratefully in Randall Thorne's bed. Eric set a glass of orange juice at his bedside.

"All the comforts of home," Paul said, extending his arms with exaggerated ease.

Suddenly an eerie howl sliced through the night. Paul shot up with a stunned expression.

"They trailed me. The dogs are down there!"

"They couldn't be," Eric said. He ran to the window and cupped his hands over his eyes. "It's okay. Relax. It's just the neighbor's schnauzer. They left him out in the yard, and he wants in."

Paul wiped a trickle of perspiration from his upper

lip. One corner of his mouth quivered slightly.

"Everything's under control," Eric said. "You've had a long day, Paul. Try to get some sleep."

Paul heaved a long sigh as his head sank into the pillow. "Thanks for everything."

As Eric turned to leave, Paul suddenly called, "Hey, I forgot about my bike! The sheriff impounded it."

"So what's a bike between friends?" Eric said. "There's a spare in the garage that you can use."

"But mine was a 10-speed Carraro. From Italy."

"You're not considering going back to Millbrook to claim it, are you?" Alison said.

"Maybe I should see a lawyer," Paul said. "To protect my interests. Remember, I'm a wanted criminal."

"Not wanted by the sheriff," Eric said. "You can be sure of that. You're the last person he wants to see again."

"I'm not sure I follow," Paul said.

"Do you think the sheriff wants his office exposed to public scrutiny?" Eric asked. "Even discounting his ties to the Nazis. If your hunch is right about the stack of wallets in his desk, he has a lot of explaining to do. I'm sure he'd rather duck the issue entirely."

Alison added, "And even if the wallets belonged to vagrants, who would be difficult to trace, an investigation would raise a lot of hot questions for the sheriff."

"He'd rather let one fish slip through the net," Eric said, "than risk a formal probe. No, my guess is you won't be hearing from the sheriff again."

"But what about the violation of my civil rights?" Paul demanded. "Am I supposed to shrug my shoulders and forget about it? That man tried to murder me."

22

"I wouldn't press it," Eric said. "At least not now, before we know the whole setup. Don't forget, you entered the situation as a reporter to investigate— But let's talk about it in the morning."

"Sure. Guess it's late," Paul yawned. "Sorry about the hassle and all the trouble I've caused."

"What hassle? What trouble?" Eric asked, leaving the room and heading for his own.

Over an early breakfast the next morning, the three decided it would be wise for Paul to stay out of circulation for a day or so. Eric offered to visit Millbrook and see what he could dig up.

"I'm going, too," Alison said.

"You are not!" Eric replied firmly. "You'll be in the way, and—"

"And what? Because I'm a girl?"

"Partly. But mostly 'cause you're pretty, in a peculiar sort of way."

"Thanks a lot!"

"You're bound to attract attention," Eric said.

"It might get rough," Paul interjected.

"This is a family argument," Alison said. "I'll thank you to keep your opinion to yourself, Paul."

"Sorry."

"Hey, that's okay, Paul. We've only been through this scene a few dozen times," Alison smiled. "Eric is ever the protective brother—even though he's younger than I am—by a full twenty minutes!"

"It's pointless to argue with her," Eric said. "If Alison's determined to string along, there's no dissuading her. You can't expect her to be sensible."

Eric offered to drive Paul home. As they went outside, Paul thanked Alison for her hospitality. "Keep your eyes open in Millbrook!" he laughed.

Eric strapped his spare bike to the top of the car, and they took off. It was a short ride to the campus and to the boarding house where Paul lived.

"Look!" Paul shouted as he climbed out of the car.

Eric followed Paul's finger pointing to a misshapen heap by the entrance to the house.

As recognition dawned, a numb sensation spread over Paul's back. There was his bicycle, the handlebars twisted like spaghetti, and the spokes resembling the ribs of a broken umbrella.

"They did a good job, the creeps," Paul said bitterly.

A blood-red swastika was painted on the front door.

# 3 • Team Preparation

"Why would anyone do such a thing?" Mrs. Tompkins, the landlady, demanded. "They must have twisted minds."

"There are a lot of weird characters on campus, Mrs. Tompkins," Eric said.

"Paul, tell me," she said, searching his face. "Has this something to do with the Ku Klux Klan?"

"If there's a Klan in Ivy," Paul said, "I've never heard of it."

"Not until now," she replied, eyeing the crudely painted swastika.

"We'll paint over it," Paul offered. "Is there a can of white paint in the garage?"

"I think so."

Mrs. Tompkins was fumbling for the garage key when the phone just inside the front door rang shrilly.

"I'll get it," Paul said and walked into the house.

He returned a minute later, his eyes angry.

25

"It was for me, Mrs. Tompkins."

Paul walked over to Eric and spoke in his ear. "I didn't recognize the man's voice. He said, 'Keep your mouth shut, nigger, or we'll string you up.' "

Eric shook his head. "That's rough, Paul."

"How would you know how it feels?" Paul asked harshly.

"Because I'm white? I can never know how it feels to be black. But I've been insulted too, and I can imagine how you feel."

"Sorry, Eric, I'm boiling with anger stored up inside me, like a vat under pressure. Sometimes it explodes at the wrong people."

"I understand," Eric said. "It looks like my hunch was right. They're telling you the matter's closed at their end; don't make any waves. They're afraid of you."

"And you're advising me to keep quiet?"

"You still can't prove a thing, Paul. It's your word against theirs. You can make things hot for the sheriff, raise doubts about his fitness for office; but you can't nail him without hard evidence. And by this time the sheriff has covered his tracks."

"What we need are fresh leads, evidence tying the sheriff to this Nazi group—or whatever they are."

"Exactly. Maybe Alison and I can uncover something. We've been playing detectives ever since we were kids."

"But this isn't amateur stuff, Eric. You're in a different league. If I take the matter to the attorney general, and he presses an investigation, it will serve notice on other Sheriff Dolans. It'll be a lesson to them all."

Eric looked at Paul's troubled face.

"I don't think you have a tight enough case," he continued. "Dolan's probably only a cog in the Nazi operation. We don't know where he figures in. Let's not let him get sidetracked. If we keep our cool, we'll develop a much stronger case."

"So long as the sheriff pays for his crimes," Paul growled.

"Paul, we need you to play along with them for now. Act as if they scared you off. If they call again, let them think you're too scared to talk."

"Just don't hurt me, Mister," Paul begged, wringing his hands in mock supplication. "I don't wants no trouble."

Eric burst into laughter.

"Ize a good nigger," Paul said, dropping to his knees.

Somehow the humor seemed forced, and Paul's mood changed abruptly. His face grew sober again. "Are you sure you want to go through with this?"

"Of course."

"These guys mean business, Eric. Deadly business."

"I know. We'll just snoop around town, see what we can dig up, and leave."

"You'll keep in touch? Well, so long. And take care of yourself!"

"Sure thing, Paul. You keep a low profile, okay?"

Eric drove through the campus, past the Student Union; along the row of stores dotting Main Street.

*By this time next year,* Eric mused, *I'll probably be thinking about coming here to school—but do I want to go to college so close to home? And at the same place my dad's a teacher?*

It was a splendid spring day. Cool air, warm sunshine—perfect weather for the spring recess. The lawns were green, and Eric heard a power mower humming. With a frown, he reminded himself that he'd have to crack some books. Midterm exams followed the vacation.

The spires of Albert Hall, housing the School of Agriculture, came into view. Midwest University was recognized for its departments of engineering and agriculture.

Eric had often stopped at Albert Hall, where his father taught agronomy. He wished his dad were in his office now so he could talk to him about what had happened to Paul Earl. He'd have some good ideas about how to get a line on the Phoenix operation those Nazis in Millbrook were running.

Eric didn't share his father's interest in agriculture. Perhaps this was due to the difference in their backgrounds. Randall Thorne had grown up on Gramps' big midwest wheat farm, where the land's fertility meant the difference between good and bad times.

Eric and Alison had been raised in this university town by their dad, with the help of Aunt Rose. Eric's goals, like his interests, were free-flowing and undefined at this point. He wasn't sure what direction his vocational interests would take. But he was sure they would not be in agronomy. Alison waffled between wanting to be a news photographer and a concert pianist, if you pinned her down to something specific. But she wasn't working very hard at either one.

Both Eric and Alison had inherited Randall Thorne's curiosity and inquisitive intelligence. The twins were still in their teens—just sixteen years old, he often reminded Aunt Rose who frequently despaired of their ever growing up to be sensible and smart "like their father."

"They're really good kids!" Mr. Thorne would say convincingly to his exasperated sister. "They'll eventually find the direction for which the Lord is gifting and preparing them. Let's give 'em a lot of love and encouragement."

"And keep praying for them 'without ceasing,' " Aunt Rose would add with a sigh.

Eric felt a flash of uncertainty. Perhaps his father would think his interest in the Phoenix affair should be left to the law enforcement specialists; that this investigation was no business for a sixteen-year-old. Especially for his twin sister!

Not that his dad wouldn't understand Eric's strong desire to help Paul Earl expose this Nazi group, but his dad would probably get counsel from his professional contacts and stay out of it himself. He was strong in letting the specialists handle matters in the areas of their specialty.

Eric preferred to get more involved in the process himself. And Alison was usually right there with him. He sensed in himself a driving determination to get into things—to become deeply and personally involved. Admittedly, this often proved to be a problem, for himself as well as for others.

Cutting across East University Avenue, Eric continued southeast for a half mile to Old Faculty Row. He stopped in front of the comfortable old white frame house at 1470 Campus Avenue. It was a sturdy, two-story structure built during the twenties when big porches were in style. At the back, a relatively new three-car garage and workshop had replaced the original woodshed and one-car garage.

Eric unlocked the front door and called Alison's name. There was no answer.

He walked to the back of the house. "Alison?"

Perhaps she had left a note. He looked in the usual places, but nothing turned up. Count on Alison to traipse off somewhere when they had important business to do.

Eric checked his watch. Ten-fifteen.

*Well, if she's not back by noon, I'm leaving without her.*

A thought began to tug at the back of his mind as impatience gave way to concern. Suppose the sheriff had succeeded in tracing Paul's movements the previous night. They might have called at the house while he was out. But this line of reasoning led to a ridiculous conclusion. Involving Alison would only increase the sheriff's risk of exposure.

No, the idea was farfetched. Still, his mind persisted in the thought. Suppose they had traced Paul to the Thorne house. They might even be grilling Alison this very minute. In Eric's imagination, he could see the desperate, cruel men at work to cover up their involvement earlier with Paul.

Eric dashed upstairs, his nerves tingling. Maybe they'd bound and gagged her and—

He burst into Alison's room. It was empty. The bed was made, and everything was in order. He searched the other rooms upstairs. Nothing was out of place.

Suddenly Eric heard the front door creak slowly open. He gasped, remembering that he'd forgotten to lock it!

"Alison?" he called.

He heard heavy steps crunching across the carpet. They weren't Alison's footsteps.

Someone was coming up the stairs.

The footsteps were coming closer.

Eric flattened himself against the wall, took a deep breath, and, counting to five, leaped out at the intruder.

A javelin flew through the air, missing Eric's nose by a whisker. At the same time, a piercing cry made his ears ring.

Eric blinked with surprise. It wasn't a javelin but a broom handle!

"Eric! You scared ten years off my life."

Eric had forgotten about Mrs. Duffy. She came every Thursday to tidy up the place.

Her face was scarlet; she was puffing and fanning herself with a large, pudgy hand. Her short-cropped henna-rinsed hair stood up like the spikes of a fence.

"Is that how you spend your time? Laying traps for overworked housekeepers?" she snorted.

"I'm sorry, Mrs. Duffy. I didn't realize it was you."

"You deliberately left the front door open."

"No, I didn't, Mrs. Duffy. It was an oversight. I thought you were a burglar. Please accept my apology."

"Well—"

"Here, have a seat."

She settled her abundant frame into a settee standing against the wall.

"I called out," Eric said, "but I guess you didn't

hear." He remembered that she was a little hard of hearing.

"You have your father's charm, Eric, and your mother's good looks."

*Your mother's good looks.* In a split second, Eric's mind flashed back over the years. A scene came before his eyes.

There was a sudden grinding of brakes, the piercing shriek of wrenched metal, a terrified cry choked off on impact.

His mother had died instantly, her car totally demolished. It was how Eric imagined the scene. In reality, he had no recollection of his mother. There was a time in his grade-school years when he refused to accept the fact of her death. He was certain that she would return someday, as if from a long trip. But in more recent times, he hadn't thought about her much—

He came to instant attention. Footsteps were padding across the hallway. Throwing caution to the wind, he barged down the stairs—and came to a sudden stop.

Alison stood at the foot of the stairs, regarding him quizzically. Her arms were loaded with bundles.

"You forgot to lock the door," she scolded.

"I know. And you forgot to leave a note. Where were you?" He started to add something about their trip to Millbrook, but remembered Mrs. Duffy. "Mrs. Duffy just arrived," he said, with a sidelong glance up the staircase.

"I figured we'd need some supplies for our—little outing."

"Good thinking," Eric said. "But time's a-wasting."

"I'll just throw some things into a bag. But first, come

32

help me fix us some sandwiches," Alison instructed.

After everything was prepared, Eric called upstairs, "Mrs. Duffy, will you please lock up when you leave?"

"All right," she answered.

"I left you some sandwiches on the kitchen table, Mrs. Duffy," Alison called out.

"Thank you, Dear. Have a good time."

Eric piled Alison's bag, his flight bag, and the picnic hamper into the car's back seat. Then they headed for Millbrook.

The possibility that they were headed on a dangerous mission came briefly to Alison's mind.

"Eric, are you certain we're doing the right thing by getting into this Phoenix matter? I mean, should we be doing our own investigating, rather than turning this over to the authorities? I'm just not sure about what we're doing."

"Yeah. I know what you mean, Twinny. But how can we let what happened to Paul be ignored? And we don't have enough information to make a case for him. That's what we have to get. Anyway, that Phoenix operation is a threat to everyone's rights—not just Paul's. Those Nazis are merchants of hate. We've got to find out more about them so the attorney general will have some good evidence of what's going on."

"The Phoenix sounds like Satan's work to me," Alison responded apprehensively. "And frankly I'm scared to be barging into it. Eric, we can't go into this without the Lord's guidance!"

"You're right about that! Doesn't the Bible say to 'watch and pray'? I'll *watch*—the road, that is. You pray."

"Eric, now stop foolin' around. This is serious!"

"Dear Father in Heaven," Alison began earnestly, "we thank You for promising to be with us always. You know that we believe we should help Paul, and that this investigation could help many others, too. And now, Lord, we need Your help—help to know what we should do and when. Thank You, Father, for hearing us and answering our prayers in the way that's best for all of us. In Jesus' name, amen."

"I'm glad we can pray about everything—and as often as we like. Seems to me I remember the Bible says to 'pray without ceasing.' " Eric's wrinkled forehead and quiet tone were familiar signals to Alison that he was deep in thought.

"Have you ever thanked the Lord that we don't have to go through some big heavenly switchboard before we get on a line with our prayers?"

"No, can't say that the idea had ever come to me just that way."

"Well, I was just thinking that we should be real glad that God is always on an open line, listening and caring about us all the time—twenty-four hours a day."

"Thanks, Alison, for reminding me of that." Eric smiled. "I have a feeling we'll be keeping that open line busy."

# 4 • Strike One

Eric filled up at a gas station and turned onto Route 36.

"We'd better check into a motel in Millbrook," Eric said as he mentally planned their strategy.

"That will be a place to meet and compare notes. The room phone will come in handy, too."

Widely spaced farms gave way to gaudy billboards as they approached Millbrook. They pulled off the highway at State Street, which appeared to be the main drag. A squint-eyed, granite-jawed replica of Clint Eastwood scowled beneath the marquee of a 1930's movie house. A loudspeaker perched above a nondescript cafe delivered a thumping volley of country-western music. And Lester Scagg, deputy sheriff, sitting idly picking his teeth, gave Eric and Alison the once-over as they drove by.

Eric turned the next corner. "Did you notice the arm of the law back there?" he asked.

35

"It's a good thing you steamed the Midwest U. decal off the bumper last week. He just might be sensitive to collegiate types."

They stopped in front of a real estate office—Alison's idea—and asked the agent if he could recommend a good place to eat and a motel, in that order.

"For purchase?" he asked, with a sly twist of his lips. He rocked back in his chair, sizing them up.

"Nope. My sister and I are just passing through," Eric replied.

"Well, if it's bed and board you kids want, I'd recommend the Inn Town Motel. Three blocks north, one block west. Tell them Harry Dalton sent you."

At the Inn Town Motel, they entered the empty lobby and punched the service bell.

A man emerged from the doorway behind the desk. He was balding, about fifty, expressionless. "Yes?"

"I'd like two connecting rooms. One's for my sister. The other's for me."

"Mr. Dalton, the realtor, recommended your motel," Alison said.

"That was nice of him. How long will you want the rooms?"

"Overnight."

"Sign the register."

As Eric wrote their names, he leaned forward casually. "Ever hear of an outfit named Phoenix?"

The man blinked. "Phoenix? Can't say I have."

He examined Eric's addition to the register. Alison noted a cameo ring on the middle finger of his left hand. Oval in shape, it depicted a bird with ornate plumage.

36

The clerk took down two room keys and handed them to Eric. "210 and 211, second floor."

"Do you have a telephone directory?" Eric asked. "Phoenix might be listed."

The man brought up a directory from behind the desk. "You have some particular interest in this Phoenix?"

"Personal," Eric said. He leafed through the pages. "No Phoenix seems to be listed," he commented with mock disappointment.

Eric and Alison took the elevator to the second floor. As the elevator opened, Eric dashed to the staircase he had noticed behind the reception desk in the lobby. Alison was at his heels. They walked halfway down, just out of sight of the desk.

The clerk was speaking in a hushed voice. Eric and Alison made out something about "two kids." The rest of the conversation was muffled by an overhead fan.

"Can't hear what he's saying," Eric whispered.

When they heard him put down the receiver, they went back upstairs. The corridor was quiet—no maids, brooms, or carpet sweepers.

They entered 210 and unlocked the connecting door. Both rooms were simply furnished, with a television set, an asthmatic air conditioner, and a single bed.

"I suspected he'd make a call," Eric said. "Too bad we couldn't hear."

"Did you notice his ring?"

"It sure wasn't a Captain Marvel decoder."

"It was a phoenix!" Alison stated with certainty.

"Who knows how a phoenix looks? It's a mythical bird."

"You don't think that was robin redbreast on that ring, do you?"

"Anyway, we've dropped our calling card. They know we're here, and that we're interested in Phoenix. The next step is ours."

"Ours? Don't you mean theirs? What makes you think they'll take a wait-and-see attitude?"

"Why shouldn't they? I can't think we appear threatening to them."

They began to make plans for the day. What better place to pick up gossip than a beauty parlor? That would be Alison's first stop.

Eric would try to find the local "hangout"—probably the cafe where they had first spotted the deputy sheriff. If it proved a dead end, he would tackle the pool hall.

They allowed for changes to suit the circumstances, but agreed to meet at the motel by five o'clock. If either of them was detained, he or she would phone.

"What if you don't return or phone?" Alison asked.

Eric's face grew rigid, his body immobile. Flashing a warning look, he cocked an ear at the door.

"Keep talking," he whispered.

"So I was telling Dad that we really ought to buy Aunt Gretchen a gift," Alison said, raising her voice. "We completely forgot her birthday last year."

"Good old Aunt Gretchen," Eric said, stalking to the door. He grasped the knob and pulled it open.

She took a startled gasp back: a blonde maid, with a motel cleaning and supply cart nearby.

"Come in," Eric said.

"Sir?" She eyed him coolly.

"You can hear better inside."

"Are you trying to pick me up? I'll report it to the manager."

"That's very good," Alison said, crossing to the door. "Have you ever acted—in amateur theatricals?"

The maid flushed. She wore heavy lipstick. A slash of blue mascara bled from the corner of each eye.

"You can leave now," Alison said, waving her off with a tone of disgust.

"Oh, yeah?" She grabbed Alison's hand and bent it back sharply.

"Ow!" An arrow of pain pierced Alison's wrist.

"Hey, you!" Eric leaped forward to break the hold.

With the palm of her hand, she gave him a shove that sent him flying halfway across the room.

Her eyes misted with pain, Alison wrenched free and stepped back into the room. She watched with fascination as the maid's hair pitched forward over her forehead, revealing a balding scalp.

"A man!" Alison exclaimed.

The "maid" shoved the hairpiece back in place and bolted down the corridor.

Eric started to follow, but Alison stopped him. "Let her—him—go." She rubbed her wrist.

"How does your hand feel?"

"The blood's starting to flow again, I think."

"Better run some cold water over it."

Alison put her hand under the tap in the bathroom.

"That creep!" Eric exploded. "I bet he came in response to the call downstairs. But why the big disguise?"

"I hope he didn't overhear our conversation about the phoenix ring," Alison said. "All this cloak-and-dagger stuff has given me an appetite." She took some sandwiches and cans of coke from the picnic hamper, and they settled down to eat.

"Do you still want to go through with this, Alison? You don't have to. You can take the car and drive back to Ivy. No demerits."

"And miss the opportunity to be recruited into Phoenix? Nothing doing."

With a sudden hunch, Eric crossed to the window. He drew back the curtain an inch. There were a few pedestrians, someone changing a tire—and a man leaning against a storefront, his face buried in a newspaper.

Standing on tiptoes, Alison stared over Eric's shoulder. "You think they put a tail on us?"

"Could be, though we must seem small fry to them."

"How often does anyone arrive in Millbrook asking about Phoenix?"

"You have a point."

The man with the newspaper glanced up at the window and lowered his gaze again.

"Is there a back exit?" Alison asked.

"We'll soon find out." Eric took Alison by the arm.

They locked the door and followed the corridor to the rear of the building.

"No outside staircase!" Alison said, disappointed.

Eric opened a window. "*Voila*! A fire escape!"

They crawled out onto the fire escape, walked down a flight of steps, unhitched a ladder leading to the street level, and found themselves in the alley. A ventilator motor hummed over the delivery entrance of the motel. A porter rolled out some garbage cans, looked around, and went back inside. He hadn't seen them.

They moved past the entrance and into a sidestreet.

# 5 • Strike Two

Together the twins circled back to the business dis
trict. From there, they went their separate ways. Eric
felt uneasy about Alison's heading off alone. But she
was no pushover. She had a good head, and would
hopefully use it.

From a common sense viewpoint, Phoenix had nothing to gain from harming her. But the organization
probably included all sorts of weird people under its
wings. Who could say what they were capable of doing?

Proceeding up State Street, Eric recognized the pool
hall from Paul's description. A few doors further up
were the cafe and the now empty bench in front of it,
where the deputy sheriff had been sitting earlier.
Through the window he noticed a number of people
eating, and decided this would be a good place to start.

He entered a wide, dimly lit room with a counter
running the length of one wall. Several people were
seated at tables, and a half dozen more were perched

at the counter. As Eric slid onto a stool, someone put a quarter in the juke box, and it began to cough rhythmically. A strobe light came on. Multicolored swirls of light swept the room in hypnotic fashion.

A man in a once-white apron and a chef's hat stood behind the counter.

"What'll ya' have?" he asked in a surly tone.

Eric ordered a Coke. A bottle of Coca-Cola and an ice-filled glass were placed in front of him on the counter.

"Ever heard the name Phoenix?" Eric asked casually.

"Phoenix, Arizona?"

"No, a sort of social club."

"In Millbrook?" The man shook his head and sauntered off to the other end of the counter. Glancing back at Eric, who lowered his gaze and pretended to be absorbed in pouring his Coke, the man motioned to the waitress. He handed her a tray, and they exchanged some whispered words. She carried it to the back of the room, where a man sat at a corner table.

The music had stopped its convulsing beat.

A strange quiet came over the place.

The man at the corner table was wearing a zippered khaki jacket. He looked to be about twenty-eight or thirty. His eyes were narrow, lips thin and tight.

The waitress spoke to him briefly. He looked over at Eric with a flat expression and emptied his glass.

The music went on again. A side door opened, and a girl stepped out with long, black hair, deep set eyes, and a toothy smile. Dressed in a sheer, deep blue blouse and full skirt, she cruised across the floor, stopping at each table, patting a customer's face, exchanging wisecracks, and whispering familiarities.

42

"How are you, Dearie?" she said, tweaking the ear of a man in a navy blue peacoat seated near Eric.

The man responded by hoisting his glass in her direction.

Her eyes moved along down the counter, stopping abruptly at Eric.

"Well, now. Who do we have here?" she cooed, gliding toward him. "Haven't we met somewhere?" She slipped her arm around his shoulders.

Eric brushed the arm away.

"Well, what d'ya know. We have an unfriendly customer here," she said, patting his face with more than a gentle touch. "I see you got rid of your girlfriend."

"You mean my sister," Eric said, trying to keep his cool.

In a sudden sweeping motion, the girl grabbed Eric's Coke and tossed it in his face. Momentarily blinded, he felt himself being shoved off the stool and pushed to the floor. He tried to stand up, but a shoe was pressed against his shoulder.

"Having trouble, Rene?" The peacoat was standing over Eric.

"You want us to work him over?" Another man glowered down at Eric.

"Hey, now, you guys—" the man from behind the counter begged, "I don't want any trouble in here. Take your quarrel outside."

The khaki jacket slowly crossed the room. "He's right. We don't want to give the place a bad reputation, do we? No, there's not gonna be any trouble."

He helped Eric to his feet and brushed him off. "You don't want any trouble, do you kid?"

Eric shook his head.

"See, no one wants any trouble. So let's break it up, okay?"

With a surly grunt, the peacoat went back to his stool at the counter. The others returned to their places.

"Thank you, boys," the girl said. "It's good to see there are still some gentlemen left to defend a lady's honor and virtue." She adjusted her hairpiece, checked her makeup in a hand mirror, and bustled out the door.

"It looked rough there for a minute," the khaki jacket said.

"I appreciate what you did," Eric said.

"Care to join me for one?"

"Sure."

He followed the man to his table.

"What'll you have?"

"A Coke," Eric said.

"A Coke!" He slapped his knees and howled in a high-pitched falsetto. "You're really hitting the big stuff, boy."

He motioned to the waitress, his expression suddenly flat and colorless.

"Yeah, Fred?" the waitress queried.

"A beer and a Coke."

The waitress went back to the counter.

"Let me give you some advice, kid. Don't antagonize Rene. She's dangerous, and her feelings are easily hurt."

Eric nodded.

"She's got her problems. But we all have our quirks. Right, kid?"

"I guess so."

"Sure. Rene is all right when you get to know her. What's your name?"

"Eric Thorne."

"Fred Purdon. Glad to meet you."

They shook hands.

The waitress returned with their drinks.

"Ella, meet Eric Thorne."

"How do you do, Eric?" The waitress gave a little nod and glided off.

"What's your interest in Phoenix?" His eyes were narrow, penetrating.

Eric tensed. "I've thought about—joining."

"What do you know about Phoenix?"

"From what I've heard, I gather it's a patriotic organization to preserve the purity of our racial stock."

"What stock is that?"

"Aryan, white, non-Semitic."

"Where did you hear about Phoenix?"

"From some guy I met."

"Some guy? Is he a member?"

"I don't think so."

"What's his name?"

"Earl—somebody."

A curious look flickered over Purdon's face. "Don't you know his full name? Where did you meet him?"

"At a party."

"Where does he live?"

"I guess he lives somewhere around Ivy."

Purdon ran an index finger around the rim of his glass. "You meet a stranger. He mentions an outfit named Phoenix, and on his say-so you drive down to Millbrook. You don't check it out further. You don't know where to join or how to join, but you drive right over. That seems odd, doesn't it?'' His eyes were as hard as blue marbles.

"Not to me."

"It would strike some people as odd. This guy Earl, what's his name, might have given you a bum steer."

"It would still be worth the trip to find out," Eric said. "Like this guy said—the country's being taken over by minority power groups. Blacks, Hispanics, Jews— they have more influence on the government than people like you and me. If that's the way it is, it makes me boil."

"You know, Eric, if this guy feels that way, how come he's not a member?"

"We didn't get into that," Eric responded.

"Well, we'll try to locate him. You have no objection, do you?"

"Of course not." Eric tried to appear calm.

"The Fuhrer welcomes new recruits—loyal, dedicated men."

Eric nearly slipped off his seat. "The Fuhrer?"

"Play your cards right, Eric, and you may get to meet him."

Eric was stunned. For a few moments, he felt as if he'd been yanked out of his own time and deposited in a different era. It was like swimming in a moving time stream, the current sweeping him between the present and 1940.

The Fuhrer? Were they all out of their minds? Eric decided not to pursue the point. *Just play along with their sick game,* he told himself. See where it leads.

It was not long before he began to wonder what he'd

gotten himself into—and how to find a way out. Perhaps he should make a run for it. Bolt out the door, race back to the motel; if Alison wasn't there, dash over to State Street and find her, find her before time ran out for both of them.

Thinking more clearly now, Eric knew he couldn't simply pick himself up and leave. What excuse could he give? He could feign illness; he really was beginning to feel very ill! But having come this far—

Eric steeled himself to keep seated. His knuckles were white from gripping the sides of his chair. Besides his fears, he felt a bit guilty about the half truths he had told Purdon about the sources of his information.

Eric weighed another consideration. If he ran off, he'd never learn about Phoenix. It would all have been for nothing. Phoenix would be alerted, put on guard. They might fold up and move their base of operations, under even tighter security.

All these considerations moved through Eric's mind with dizzying speed.

"Anything the matter?" Purdon asked.

"No, why?"

"Your mind seemed to be elsewhere. You don't look good. Is the drink too strong for you?" He laughed his long, unsettling hyena laugh.

"I guess so, not enough ice."

Purdon produced another long howl. "I like your sense of humor, kid—but back to business. I can take you to headquarters. We can go now. I'll drive you."

"Is it far?"

"Not too far."

He slapped some bills on the table. "It's on me, kid.

I'll be right back.'' He stood up and walked into the men's room.

This is your chance to get out. The thought forced itself into Eric's mind. Involuntarily, his eyes flicked to the door.

Everybody was staring at him. Maybe if he just nonchalantly walked out—

He rose slightly. As he did so, several others turned toward the door, blocking his way. They reminded Eric of bald eagles: hunched, ready to pounce, to savage their prey.

Eric eased back in his chair. The men relaxed, tension visibly draining. Their jaws were still set, however, their limbs still fixed in an attitude of readiness. And their eyes—there was something about them. A look of chronic wariness and suspicion.

Purdon returned and Eric followed him to the door. As they passed the counter, he gave a slight wave to the waitress. One of the men pushed himself away from a table and walked to the opposite side of the room.

Behind him, Eric heard the clink of a coin. As he stepped out into the sunlight, a raspy voice began to whisper into the pay phone.

# 6 • Gestapo Interrogation

Purdon drove in tight lipped silence. His amiability in the cafe had vanished. He seemed morose and preoccupied.

"Is something bothering you?" Eric asked.

"Why should something be bothering me?"

"I don't know. You seem very serious."

"Well, it's an auspicious occasion. It isn't every day I recruit another Aryan, white, non-Semitic candidate." He slapped Eric's knee and went off into a gale of laughter.

The car sped on.

"Aren't we past the city limits?" Eric asked.

Purdon remained silent.

"What town is this?" Eric asked.

"Relax, kid. Stop worrying."

"I'm just curious."

A motorcycle raced up behind them.

"Hey look, kid, we got our own police escort."

The motorcycle came up level with the car. Lester Scagg, the deputy sheriff, gave a nod of greeting. "How's it going, Fred?"

"Can't complain."

"Who's that?" Scagg jerked a finger at Eric.

"This is Eric Thorne."

"Where are you from, Eric?"

"Professional curiosity," Purdon said with a smirk.

"Ivy," Eric answered.

"Central or Riverside?"

Eric thought fast. There were two high schools in Ivy. The bulk of Central High's students came from University faculty families and the business community. There was an intense and often unfriendly rivalry between the two schools. Eric and Alison had gone to Central.

"Riverside," Eric answered.

Scagg seemed pleased. "Going to college?"

"I might," Eric said.

It was the wrong answer. He realized that immediately. Scagg's jaw tightened slightly.

"But I'll probably take up a trade," Eric added hastily. "TV repair or photography most likely."

Scagg nodded. "See you later." He buzzed on past them.

"Les is a good man," Purdon said.

"From the Millbrook Sheriff's Department, isn't he?"

"Yeah."

"Isn't he outside his jurisdiction here?"

"Les doesn't worry about jurisdictions. A guy tangles with Les, he ends up with a broken arm."

50

"Is he one of us?"

"What do you think?" He poked Eric in the ribs.

They were coming into a wooded area. It was miles since they'd seen a diner, a gas station, or a farmhouse. A squirrel suddenly hopped out into the road. Purdon pushed down on the accelerator, his eyes flickering with a wild, hungry flame. The car was headed straight for the animal.

Eric wanted to grab the wheel, but knew it would be taken as a sign of weakness. That would be fatal to his plans. He squeezed back into his seat, teeth clenched, praying the animal would dodge away in time. The squirrel turned its eyes directly on the car and, in a sudden burst of speed, leaped to safety, inches from the front bumper. With a bound, it was in the bushes, the car rocketing past.

Purdon's disappointment quickly turned to anger. "We almost got him!"

He went on to relate how, as a child, he took particular pleasure in skinning polecats alive. He described the process in great detail. Eric fought a pang of nausea. He looked out the window and prayed silently that God would bring him safely through the danger he knew he was in with this cruel maniac.

They turned onto a bumpy dirt road past a stretch of old shacks and an abandoned construction site. The road continued a few miles, curving into a gloomy thoroughfare lined with factories and warehouses.

Purdon drew up at a warehouse that carried the name PARAGON in large block letters.

"I'll have to blindfold you the rest of the way." Reaching into the glove compartment, he withdrew a black handkerchief and wound it tightly around Eric's eyes.

The car started up, moving in the same direction for what Eric judged to be a mile. Then he felt the car follow a winding, twisting route that left him thoroughly disoriented. He tried to pick out some sounds from the confusing welter of background noises. The only one he could distinguish was a rhythmic clacking-and-creaking noise. It sounded familiar, though he couldn't place it. Further along, he heard a train whistle, and the sound of a locomotive fading into the distance.

After driving for another five minutes or so, Purdon stopped. "We get out here," he said.

Eric heard the door on his side open. Purdon was getting out the other side. Footsteps circled the car. Then Purdon's hand was on Eric's elbow, leading him out of the car.

"Watch the curb."

Eric stepped blindly up to the curb, was steered left for nine paces, then told to halt and turn right. He heard a clinking sound. Keys. Purdon was turning a lock. It must be a heavy steel door: Eric heard it heave ponderously, with a grating sound.

He felt the blindfold loosened, untied; then it was off. Eric rubbed his eyes with relief. They entered a large, dimly lit space that exuded an unpleasant musty smell. The windows were barred, and Eric wondered when the place had last been aired. Large drum-shaped cartons lined the walls. Their footsteps echoed on the bare wooden floors.

"Is this headquarters?" Eric asked, posing an excited interest.

"We don't want to advertise the place," Purdon answered. "It's our secret meeting place and armory. The warehouse is a front."

A warehouse. It had slipped out. Eric pretended not to notice. Purdon colored, aware of his blunder.

Purdon conducted him to the back of the room, then tapped on a rear door in a repetitive one-two rhythm. The door slid open.

They entered a medium-sized room bathed in fluorescent light. The back wall was draped with a huge red tapestry of flags bearing the Nazi swastika. Above the flags were two crossed swords and a portrait of Adolf Hitler.

World War II souvenirs covered the other walls: helmets, bayonets, Lugers, emblems, posters, coins, medals, brass buttons, swagger sticks, armbands, and enlarged photographs of Hitler's inner circle: Eva Braun, Goering, Himmler, Goebbels, Eichmann, and others. There were pictures of German soldiers locked in tight ranks goose-stepping across Europe. And a sign read ARBEIT MACHT FREI. "Work creates freedom." Eric recalled that this was the sign which hung over the entrance to the concentration camps he had heard about.

A sudden surge of military music engulfed the room. Cymbals crashed and trumpets blared. Eric wondered who was supplying the sound effects.

After a few minutes, the volume dropped to an austere, measured beat. A wall panel swung open, and four men marched into the room. They were wearing crisp Nazi uniforms with high jackboots and military caps. Standing before Eric were four of the generals in the photographs: Goebbels, Himmler, Goering, and Heydrich.

Eric had read about them in history books. Hadn't they all died in the forties? Granted, their faces were older and wrinkled—but they were clearly recognizable. They were not faces one soon forgot.

Plastic surgery? A possibility. Eric had little time to mull it over, for they were pressing around him, studying him with greedy interest, like some prize specimen.

"You," Goebbels rapped out, "what is your name?"

Eric swallowed.

"Quick, your name." The point of a swagger stick prodded Eric's shoulder.

"Eric Thorne."

He was a short runt of a man, Eric thought, but with a commanding presence that made him seem taller.

"What is your *real* name?"

"That is my real name." Eric was relieved that he hadn't used a false identity. They would have checked it out. A phony address would not have borne scrutiny.

"Show me your identity papers."

He didn't say "ID." He spoke like the Gestapo in a 1940's movie.

Eric showed him his driver's license, and Social Security card. Goebbels inspected them and handed them to the others. He went to a desk and pulled out a pen and a pad of paper.

"Sign your name," he told Eric.

Eric wrote his signature, and the Nazis compared it with the signature on the documents.

"Why did you say you went to Riverside High School?" Himmler asked.

The deputy must have reported their conversation. Had they already checked on his high school? How could they have done it so quickly? Should he stick with the story he gave Les Scagg?

"Because I thought if I told him I attended Central High, it would prejudice him against me."

"How do you know Les' prejudices?"

"I don't. It's a matter of intuition."

Heydrich took over. "You secured information about Les; you looked up his background before coming to Millbrook."

"No, I didn't." Eric protested. "He just seemed the type who resents education."

"A low life, in other words."

"I'm not saying that. I just didn't want to start out on the wrong foot with him by emphasizing a different social background. There's a kind of feud between the two schools."

"Whatever the reason, you lied to us." Heydrich's face was rigid.

"Not to you, to Les. I didn't know he was a member. It didn't seem of any consequence what I told him. He was just cruising along on his motorcycle, making conversation."

Heydrich went to the desk and took out a large square book. Eric recognized it immediately. The Central High Yearbook.

Heydrich leafed through the pages, stopping at T. "Is this your picture?" he asked.

"Yes." It was Eric's sophomore class photo.

"Where did you hear of us?" Heydrich asked.

Eric had a sinking sensation. It was the question he

most dreaded. "I told Fred. He knows all about it."

Purdon was sitting on the desk, legs crossed, a vapid smile on his lips. He didn't volunteer a word.

"Fred has communicated the salient facts to us."

"How? He was with me all the time," Eric blurted.

"All the time? You're not very observant."

"Oh." Eric remembered. All but the time he went to the men's room.

"We want to hear it from your lips," Heydrich pursued.

"I met a fellow in Ivy. At a party. His name was— Earl something. Earl. That part I'm sure about."

"Is he a resident of Ivy?"

"I guess."

"You guess? You're not certain? Didn't you consider it prudent to corroborate his information? Do you believe everything regardless of its source?"

"Of course not."

"You're not even sure Earl was his real name, are you?"

Eric reddened. His head began to throb. "I don't ask people to prove they are who they say they are."

"You take people on face value?"

"Not always. This Earl seemed genuine to me. He said he'd like to join Phoenix."

"Yet this—person—never attempted to join."

"You'd have to ask him about that."

"How do we go about it?" Himmler asked. "There are many Earls in Ivy. We have scrutinized the phone directory and the city registry in Ivy's municipal building."

Eric swallowed hard.

56

"Actually, he could be from some nearby town. Besides, he's young; he probably lives with his parents. There wouldn't necessarily be a listing under his own name."

"We thought of that. But until you produce this individual, your story is suspect."

"A question mark hangs over your head, Eric Thorne," Goering said.

"You see, you slipped up, kid," Purdon said, hopping off the desk. "Oh, you're good, but not good enough."

"I don't know what you mean," Eric blurted.

"How did your friend, Earl, obtain the name Phoenix?" Goebbels asked. "It's not the public name of our organization. You thought it was. It's a secret code name we use only among ourselves. It doesn't circulate."

The five men were staring hard, intimidatingly, waiting for an answer.

An overhead light beamed into Eric's eyes, burning and blurring his vision.

"Keep your eyes open," Goebbels ordered.

Eric forced his lids apart, but they kept closing. He was blinded by a shower of dazzling light. Eric realized it was an old Gestapo interrogation technique designed to increase his vulnerability. It was working, too, working with incredible ease. It became difficult for him to think. His tongue felt as dry as sandpaper. He'd forgotten the last question. What was the last question? His thoughts were melting together like candle wax.

Goebbels was tapping his fingers impatiently.

They were waiting for an answer.

58

# 7 • *Room Search*

Alison stared helplessly at the telephone, her face tight with worry. It was past five, and Eric had promised to phone if he was detained. It was careless of them not to have worked out a contingency plan in case one of them failed to phone. As she recalled, they were about to discuss it when the "maid" interrupted them.

Five-twenty, and she was beside herself with impatience. She knew Eric would call if he were able. It was not something he would forget. But, she tried to reassure herself, he might be in a situation where it was inconvenient. Or awkward. Perhaps he wasn't located near a phone. If he had succeeded in making contact with Phoenix, they might have taken him somewhere. That was the most likely possibility. But where?

The minutes dragged. Five-thirty. What if Eric was hurt, in need of help? Alison's mind leapt to the gravest possibilities. She pictured him lying in a deserted road, arms and legs twisted grotesquely beneath him. Or bound and gagged, feet weighted, sinking to the bottom of—no, she must control her thoughts. She mustn't let her imagination get the best of her. She had to remain calm, cool—but it was difficult!

Hadn't they prayed for God's guidance in doing what they believed was right? Her nerves were taut, and restlessness repeatedly carried her across the room and back. It was not knowing, not having anything to do except wait. While she waited and paced the room, she prayed, "Lord, please help Eric, wherever he is."

Five-fifty. The phone rang. Alison snatched it up. Wrong number! "No, this is not room 319!"

She had to talk to someone. If only Dad were home. Aunt Rose? She was gone, too. Anyway, she didn't want to worry her.

Paul! Of course. But what was his number? She'd memorized it. 453-9873: or was it 9872? Yes, that was it. She sprang to the phone. Wait, she mustn't phone from the motel. They might listen in. Calls were relayed through the switchboard. She'd have to use a pay phone. But if she went outside, she might miss Eric's call. She stood undecided—

It was past six. She would have to chance it. If Eric called while she was out, the switchboard operator would probably leave a message. Even if they were suspicious of Eric and Alison.

She glanced out the window. The street was dark. A light van rolled by. A couple strolled past, hands entwined. The man with the newspaper might be watching from some shadowy recess. She stepped away from the window. She hadn't spotted him when she returned from the beauty parlor. He'd probably gone.

She put on a sweater, locked the door, and took the elevator down to the lobby. The desk clerk glanced up as she passed him. But she went out without a word, walking hurriedly down the street.

A drug store stood on the corner. She looked inside. There were two phone booths near the door. She stepped inside one of them, and swung the door closed. She was about to deposit a coin, when a man sitting at the lunch counter stood up and walked in her direction. He was about forty, thin, medium height, wearing a tired tan suit. His flat brown hair was parted in the center. The man with the newspaper!

He entered the booth behind Alison. From the corner of her eye, Alison noticed that he didn't dial the phone or even fish for a coin. He just sat, sat and stared at Alison.

She sprang up, swung back the folding door and ran into the street. As she glanced back, his lips parted in a grin. She raced wildly down the street.

Alison turned at the first corner and crossed diagonally to a luncheonette. A couple of people were chatting at the counter. A single phone booth stood at the rear of the store. She entered the booth and waited. No one followed her into the store. Alison deposited a dime and dialed Paul's number. The operator requested an additional thirty-five cents. Alison fed the phone; she heard a ring at the other end of the line.

"Hello."

"Paul, this is Alison. How are you feeling?"

"A lot better now. How are you and Eric?"

"We're in Millbrook."

"Did something come up?"

"Yes." She quickly summarized everything that had happened since they arrived. "And Eric was supposed to be back at the motel by five or phone if he couldn't make it."

"So they've got him," he said, with a note of finality.

"Not necessarily, Paul. It might be inconvenient for him to call now." Her voice lacked conviction.

"They've got him, Alison. Let's face the facts. Eric would find a way to call if it were possible."

"What should I do? Call the police?"

"What police? The *Millbrook* police?"

"I see your point. They're probably in cahoots with the Nazis."

"I'm coming over, Alison."

"Paul, you mustn't! Are you crazy? They'll spot you within a mile of Millbrook and throw you in the slammer again."

"I'll take my chances. At night I have protective coloration—natural camouflage. I got Eric and you into this. I feel responsible."

"Paul, there's nothing for you to atone for. We went into this with our eyes wide open."

"I'm leaving now, Alison."

"Stay away! This time they'll make dog food out of you. Don't be a hero or a dead martyr."

"You can't ask me to sit on my haunches—and do nothing."

"What could you possibly accomplish in Millbrook?"

"I'll go back to the pool hall and wring the truth out of those guys."

"With your bare hands? One person against a whole gang? Be sensible."

"This time I'll be armed. The element of surprise will be on my side."

"Paul, you're not a violent person. Don't let them force you to become like them. They'll smash you. To them violence is a way of life. They're professionals."

"Blacks have always had to fight for their lives and values. Every generation inherits that struggle. You don't understand that, Alison, because you come from a nice white, middle-class culture where Mommy tucks you in at night and makes you feel safe."

"My mother died when I was two." Alison felt tears spring to her eyes. Memories washed over her, and a void opened up—the terrible emptiness left by her mother's death.

"I'm sorry, kid. I'm sorry," Paul stumbled. "I forgot." His voice broke.

A silence fell between them. Neither attempted to speak.

Presently, Paul asked, "You really want me to remain here?"

"Yes. I don't see what you can accomplish, Paul. Forfeiting your life won't bring back Eric—if something's happened to him. Eric knew the risks involved."

"Maybe he'll still pull it off, Alison. Eric's resourceful. I wouldn't sell him short."

"I'll head back to the motel and wait."

"I suggest you come home now, Alison. Tomorrow we can go to the FBI and tell them our story. Or we can call them tonight."

"We don't have much of a case against anyone. We

don't know who the ringleaders are. We don't know who Eric saw today. All we can report are vague rumors and suspicions. Hearsay evidence.''

"I'll tell them about the sheriff.''

"We have no evidence he's even tied up with the Nazis. Nothing tangible to show the FBI.''

"We have to do something. The FBI is our last and only hope. Kidnapping is a federal offense. It falls within their jurisdiction.''

"All right, if Eric's not back by morning, I'll come back to Ivy.''

"I think you oughta come now.''

"Tomorrow morning, Paul. If the Nazis were going to harm me, they'd have done it by now.''

"Call me if you hear from Eric. Or if there's any trouble. Promise?''

"I promise.''

"And ring me before you leave tomorrow. Okay?''

"Right. See you tomorrow.'' She hung up.

Alison sat a few moments composing herself, then left the store and started back. What had she hoped to accomplish by phoning Paul? He offered his help and she refused it. What else could he have done? He was prepared to put his life on the line. You couldn't ask more of a person. She'd only succeeded in upsetting him by venting her own fears. But she did feel better for having talked to someone.

She glanced carefully about the street. There was no sign of the man in the tan suit. But he could still pop out of a doorway. Alison hugged the curb.

She was relieved to see a middle-aged couple walking in the same direction, and fell into step behind them.

64

Accompanied by her unwitting chaperons, she made her way back to the motel.

The clerk was off duty, and a slim young man with unruly hair and an advanced case of acne stood behind the desk. Alison caught him eyeing her with more than professional interest as she crossed the lobby.

She asked whether she had received any calls. He glanced inside her box.

"Nope, nothing here."

She rode up in the elevator. As she approached her room, she thought she heard a faint scurrying inside. She tried the doorknob. It was locked. Listening at the door, she concluded that she must have been mistaken. Nerves, she thought. She unlocked the door and entered.

BANG!

There was no mistaking *that* sound. Someone had slammed a door. Someone in a hurry to leave. It had come from Eric's room.

She ran into the hall. It was empty. Obviously the intruder had waited for Alison to enter, and timed his departure perfectly. Was it the man in tan?

She examined her room. Nothing was out of place. But closer inspection revealed some telltale signs of a stranger's presence: a hairbrush upside down, a bureau drawer slightly open, a burnt match on the floor. Neither Alison nor Eric smoked.

She opened her bag. The clothing was rearranged. Someone had gone over the contents thoroughly, but nothing was taken.

The connecting door to Eric's room was open. She looked inside. Again, there were no obvious signs of a search. But Alison bet the intruder had gone over every inch of the room. Unless she had interrupted him.

This was not the work of a common hotel thief. Alison hated to spend another moment in the place. But despite her feelings, she had to remain. There was nothing to do except wait, and hope Eric would phone.

She took a chair and jammed it under the doorknob. It would make turning the knob difficult. If anyone knocked the chair over, the noise would give her a moment's warning. A moment to scream, hoping to scare off the intruder.

She took the precaution of propping a chair against Eric's door too, since there was a common access. Then Alison lay back in bed, staring at the phone. Still restless, she got up and checked the dial tone. It was in perfect working order. But the phone was mute. It might as well be dead.

Dead. The word sent a shock through her.

Eric, why don't you phone?

"Lord, please let him phone. Please keep my brother safe."

# 8 • The Interrogation Continues

The overhead light burned into Eric's eyes. He lifted a protective arm, but Goering struck it down.

"I asked you about Phoenix," Goebbels said.

"What was the question?" Eric's head was humming.

"Phoenix is a secret code name. Where did you hear about it?"

"Earl used the name."

"Your old friend Earl!" Goering spat on the floor.

Eric persisted with his story. "Maybe he heard it from a member. You're a propaganda expert, General Goebbels. You know how things leak out and begin to circulate."

Goebbels gave a dry laugh. "He's trying to beat me at my own game. It is possible that one of our members used the name inadvertently," he conceded.

"And it is also possible," he continued, "that Earl—this phantom Earl—is an undercover agent. As you may be," Goering said, his heavy jowls trembling with anger.

Eric forced himself to laugh. The laughter was louder than he expected, with a ring of hysteria. "Look, I realize you're testing me. It's wise to be suspicious of any prospective member. But would the FBI be stupid enough to recruit a dumb amateur like me?"

"He's holding back," Goering said. "His Earl story reeks of rotten limburger."

"He may have reasons for inventing Earl," Goebbels said, "but he is too unpolished for an agent."

Eric breathed an inward sigh of relief.

"He could be in the employ of some other agency," Himmler said.

"I'm not," Eric protested.

"No, I think he came here on his own initiative," Goebbels said. "Whether he can be trusted is an entirely different question."

"I came here to see about joining the Party," Eric said. "All my life I've been intrigued by Adolf Hitler. He's a hero, an idol. Being a member of the Party could give my life new meaning, purpose, direction. You have no reason to mistrust me. I could prove my trustworthiness to you."

"Who is the girl at the motel?" Goering asked. He looked at Eric through narrowly mocking eyes.

"My sister Alison."

"A tart you picked up!" Goering barked.

Eric's eyes flared angrily. He sprang to his feet, his face a white mask of indignation. "She's my twin sister!"

Heydrich shoved him back in the chair.

"Why did you bring her?" Goebbels asked.

"I couldn't shake her. I made the mistake of telling

her I was taking a ride to Millbrook, and she insisted on coming along.''

"What reason did you give her for your trip?"

"I said I wanted to do some research—a history project."

"Didn't she ask for more details?"

"That seemed to satisfy her. I dropped her off at a beauty parlor while I went to work on my project."

"When did you say you would be back?"

"About five."

Goebbels looked at his watch. It was close to seven. "She'll be worried about you. She would expect you to phone, wouldn't she?"

"Yes."

"Stand up," Goebbels ordered. "There's a phone in the back room."

Eric's legs felt weak and he was slightly dizzy.

"You will tell your sister you are making progress on your research, that you will return to the motel within a few hours."

"To the motel!" They know where Alison is! Eric's heart gave a leap. "Return within a few hours!" He followed Goebbels into a small room with a desk in the corner. Without a word, Goebbels turned and left the room, closing the door behind him.

They must be listening in on an extension, Eric thought. He hoped Alison wouldn't blurt something out that would give them away.

He rang the motel and asked for Alison's room. She answered on the first ring. "Hello?"

Eric spoke in a slurred, drunken voice. "Hello, Allie, old girl."

"Eric?"

"None other."

"Sounds like you're drunk! What's the matter with you?"

"I stopped to have a few with the boys. Oliver, Chuck, Ellery. You know, the old gang."

Alison was perplexed. Eric didn't drink. He didn't belong to a gang. And she had never heard of Oliver or Chuck—the Nazis must be monitoring his call!

"Well, I'm glad one of us is having fun," Alison said. "I'm stuck at the motel. When will you be back?"

"In a few hours. Shouldn't be long."

"I'll expect you soon then?" She needed reassurance.

"Sure thing." He hung up.

Goebbels opened the door. "Why did you act drunk?"

"You were listening in?"

"You knew we were. Answer my question."

"Stopping for a little drink—or two—explains why I didn't phone earlier."

Goebbels smiled. He seemed satisfied. He led Eric back to the other room and pushed him into the chair. The overhead light came on again, harsh and glaring.

"Look, I've had enough of this," Eric said angrily. "I didn't come here to be cross-examined. I came of my own free will."

"We will tell you when you have had enough. You want to be a Nazi? You will learn to take orders without question."

"Then you're accepting me as a member?"

"Not so fast. There are points we must clear up. Maintaining the ridiculous fiction about this Earl somebody will make it difficult for you. You may be shield-

70

ing someone else whose identity you're loathe to reveal. There may be other reasons for this fabrication. Whatever they are, it would be wise to make a clean breast of it."

Eric looked Goebbels in the eye, but made no reply.

"All right, stick with your story," Goebbels said. "You may have good reason for this deception. But you will have to prove yourself in a more convincing fashion than other recruits whose sponsors are familiar to us. God help you if we discover you're a spy—" He left the rest of the sentence unfinished, but there was no doubt in Eric's mind as to what the consequences would be.

"So you're admitting me on a provisional basis?"

"We'll have to run a thorough check on your background first."

"Will it take long?"

"We will see," Goebbels said. "Everything in its time. As the English say, patience is a virtue."

Goering drew his comrades over to one side, out of earshot. "I still think he's a lying dog and ought to be eliminated." Goering snarled the words.

"There is time for that—if the situation warrants. Let him play out his string; see where it leads."

"I agree," Himmler said. "He may not be acting alone. If others are involved, he'll lead us to them."

"I trust him as little as you," Heydrich said, laying a hand on Goering's shoulder. "But there's no hurry. He can't hurt us. Where can he run? Where can he hide? He cannot hope to elude us. Right, Fred?"

Purdon flashed a tobacco-stained smile. If Eric gave them the slip, he would be chosen to hunt him down. Anticipation made his mouth water.

They returned to Eric.

"There is one other question," Goebbels said.

Eric tensed. Goebbels' questions were like darts.

"Why didn't you comment on our appearance?"

"I don't understand," Eric said.

"We appear before you as German generals familiar from history books. Correct?"

"Yes."

"They are dead. Goebbels, Goering, Himmler, Heydrich."

"I thought they were dead, before I met you."

"And now you think they're alive?"

"Yes—I mean no. I don't know what to think any more."

"They are dead, young man," Goebbels said. "You are too easily persuaded by your senses. You must learn skepticism, cynicism. Become hard if you want to be a good Nazi."

Goebbels slowly pulled the edge of a flesh-tinted, skintight mask from his neck. "You see?" He let it fall back invisibly into place. "How easy it was to fool you."

They were fiendishly clever masks. Shining a light in his eyes had aided their masquerade, Eric realized.

"We are plaster saints," Himmler said, "borrowing the glory of our predecessors. But for a purpose—"

"If you earn our trust, we will reveal our true identities to you," Heydrich said.

"If," Goering added, with glowering menace. "If!"

# 9 • Bugged

Some unusual sound had cut through Alison's sleep. Jerked awake, she was dimly aware of a clicking noise.

After receiving Eric's call, she had dozed off from nervous exhaustion. It was a troubled sleep, and she was easily roused.

*Click-click, click-click.*

Her eyes whipped wide open. It seemed to be coming from Eric's room. Alison fought to clear her senses. Though not fully awake, she climbed out of bed and padded cat-footed to the door connecting their rooms. She hung on the threshold, listening.

The doorknob was shaking. Alison took a sharp intake of air. Someone was trying to get in. The chair was wedged solid against the knob, resisting the efforts to force it. But the knob kept rattling, and it was slowly beginning to turn.

Alison grabbed the first object within reach—an empty vase. Holding it high, she crossed to the door.

73

The chair was wobbling, teetering back and forth. Alison flattened herself against the wall. With a sudden explosion, the chair fell back, the door gave in, and a man stepped into the room. Alison caught a glimpse of a white shirt. For a moment it appeared to hang suspended against the moonlit pane. Then a face whose features were hidden by darkness turned in her direction. Alison swung the vase.

"Alison! What are you doing?"

The light snapped on. The vase crashed to the floor.

Eric stood owl-eyed with surprise.

"Eric!" She ran into his arms with a surge of relief.

"I couldn't open the door. Did you shove something against it?" His eyes fell on the chair, and understanding broke over his face.

"We had a burglar while I was out. He ransacked the place, but nothing's missing. I thought he was paying us a return call."

Eric glanced about the room. Before Alison could say another word, he put a finger to his lips.

Eric whispered into Alison's ear, "Our burglar may have planted a bug."

"Let's make sure the burglar didn't take anything," Eric said loudly for the benefit of anyone who might be recording their conversation.

He pulled down the window shades and inspected everything in sight, then stood up on a chair to examine the light fixture. Taped to the inside of the canopy was a small metallic instrument.

Eric motioned for Alison to follow him into her room. He repeated the entire operation, uncovering a second bug in the same location in Alison's room.

"I guess you're right, Alison. Nothing was taken. I'm going to wash up."

He gestured to Alison to follow him into the bathroom. Turning the shower on full force, Eric said, "We can talk safely now. They'll never hear us."

"What happened to you?" Alison asked.

Eric described his meeting with Fred Purdon in the cafe, Rene, and the fight.

"It's lucky you got out in one piece," Alison said, with a shudder.

"That was just the preliminary bout," Eric said. He went on to relate his encounter with the four bogus generals.

"You ought to have seen them, Ali. They gave a perfect performance. The whole atmosphere of the place made it actually seem real."

"How horrible! What people, strutting around in uniform, intimidating raw recruits."

"They're sadists. That's what they are. I got the full treatment because my answers left them unsatisfied. The Earl somebody name I used couldn't be confirmed. That was the major flaw in my story. But it's so close to the truth it may eventually give us away. Fortunately it also couldn't be disproved."

"They were suspicious of you, but they still felt you were promising material? Aha! I always knew you were a Nazi at heart!"

Eric playfully splashed water on Alison.

"Hey! I just had a shampoo and haircut. You're ruining my new hairdo." She retaliated by aiming the shower at him.

"Okay, enough, enough. I give up," Eric screamed.

They toweled themselves dry and sat down on the edge of the bathtub.

"So how did your day go?" Eric asked.

"Uneventful, except for the burglar. Oh yes, I met our friend, the guy with the newspaper."

"Tan suit?"

"None other. He didn't do anything, just tried to eavesdrop on a telephone conversation."

"In the motel?"

"No, outside."

"Who did you phone?"

"Paul."

"Why?"

"I was scared when you didn't call. I waited till six."

Eric rubbed his chin thoroughly. "I expect it was that man in tan that rifled our rooms. He waited all day for an opportunity, and when you ducked out, he doubled back here."

"That's how I figure it," Alison said. "I'm sure he didn't find anything of interest, though."

"Did you collect any information in the beauty parlor?"

"The usual gossip about who was dating who, who was getting married or unmarried. I tried to open the subject of the Nazis, but they drew a curtain on the subject."

"Wouldn't tumble, huh?"

"Except to hint that things are popping and that the Fuhrer will put the place on the map."

"The Fuhrer! Why didn't you mention him before? Did you get a description?"

"No. They didn't say anything beyond the fact that he was giving a talk next week, and I had to see him in person. I gather he's a magnetic personality."

"Like old Adolf himself. Purdon told me that if I played my cards right, I'd get to meet him."

"Apparently he's a rather mysterious subject, though. I couldn't discover anything else about him."

"They're afraid of saying the wrong thing. Insult the Fuhrer—even innocently—and you're *kaput*." Eric tightened an imaginary noose around his neck. "The Nazis had a network of informers during World War II, you know. Kids would turn in their own parents. That's how Hitler maintained power, through terror."

"Who would want to live in a country dominated by such fear?"

"The Germans had no choice once Hitler assumed command. He clamped a stranglehold on the country. Citizens feared for their lives and for their families. Panic kept everyone in line."

"Add to that, constant war hysteria whipped up by patriotic appeals to national pride."

Eric and Alison paused in their thoughts. Then Eric returned to their immediate problem.

"What did Paul have to say?"

"He wanted to charge into Millbrook, guns blazing, to rescue you."

"That's just like Paul. He'd do that for a friend, or for the right cause, risk his life. I'm glad you stopped him."

"Frankly, if I had thought he could have saved you, I wouldn't have lifted a finger to stop him. But it was a foolish, noble, heroic, and ultimately pointless gesture, doomed to fail. Paul knew it. But he was willing to take the odds.''

"The sheriff and Scagg—"

"Who's Scagg?"

"His deputy. They'd love to have a second shot at Paul.''

"I promised to phone him, to let him know you're safe.''

"Where from? Not the motel.''

"No, from a phone booth, same as before.''

"They probably have a tail on me, Alison. It would look suspicious if you went out now to phone. They'd guess you were afraid of being overheard in the motel. The obvious conclusion: you left to contact a third party to this affair.''

"But I promised Paul I'd call. He's worried.''

"Don't you think I realize that? But there just isn't any safe way to do it.''

"We could use the fire escape. It worked this afternoon.''

"Too risky. Circumstances are different. We'll just have to stay put until tomorrow, and call Paul when we get back to Ivy.''

"The Nazis are letting you go free? Just like that?''

"Not exactly. They know where I live. They have my address. They'll keep tabs on me. We can be certain of that.''

"Did they make any future arrangements with you?''

"On the way back Purdon said they'll contact me next week. If everything checks out.''

"And if it doesn't?''

"Then I had the shortest Nazi career in history.''

# 10 • Tailed

The desk clerk looked up sharply as Eric and Alison stepped out of the elevator. It was eight o'clock in the morning.

"We're checking out," Eric said, handing him the keys.

"The security in this place could be improved," Alison observed wryly.

"What do you mean?"

"Skip it," Eric said. He paid the bill, and they left.

They drove up State Street and turned onto Route 36. It was a pleasant day, the highway shimmering in the morning sun.

Eric and Alison shared unspoken thoughts and common emotions. Each felt grateful to God that they were leaving Millbrook in one piece. They had a sense of accomplishment, of a mission successfully completed. The trip had been exploratory. They had made contacts, now it was a matter of waiting to see what developed. Despite the feeling of achievement, however, a sense of foreboding clouded the future, a foreboding that neither cared to express. They had touched evil in Millbrook, and its dark presence lingered with them as they rode back to Ivy.

Eric gave a groan as he glanced over his shoulder.

"What's the matter?"

He adjusted the rearview mirror. A motorcycle was coming up fast behind them.

"The police?" Alison asked.

"The deputy."

Scagg pulled up beside them. Eric pulled the car over.

"Good morning, deputy," Eric said.

"Morning, Central. Leaving without saying good-bye? I feel slighted."

"No offense intended," Eric answered. "I figured you were out rounding up criminals."

"You haven't introduced me to the doll."

"My twin sister, Alison. Meet Lester Scagg."

"Pleased to meet you," Alison said.

"Not as pleased as I am," Scagg replied. "Sure you won't stay a little longer?"

"Some other time."

Scagg shifted his attention to Eric. "What's the hurry, Central?"

"I don't want to strain Millbrook's hospitality."

"Oh we're very hospitable people. Why did you tell me you went to Riverside?"

"Perhaps I never liked it at Central," Eric said. "It was my father's idea to go there."

"You talk like a Central High student. All that

la-de-da psychology stuff. To a simple guy like me, you told a lie, plain and simple."

"If I'd gone to Riverside, I wouldn't have had to lie. That's how things work out sometimes."

"That makes sense. Gotta go now. See you around, Central. You too, Alison."

He made a wide U-turn and sped off.

As Eric started the car, Alison said, "You were a big hit with Scagg."

"My natural Central charm. You made a bigger hit."

Alison laughed, then turned pensive and sank back into her seat.

Ivy was a welcome sight. As Eric drove through its tree-lined streets, Millbrook seemed like a distant mirage. Yet Eric had seen it with his own eyes. There was a base of Nazi operations, just a few miles away!

They were riding up Twelfth Street when they saw the patrol car. It was parked in front of their house. Mrs. Duffy, the housekeeper, burst out the door, trailed by a policeman. She was breathing hard and fanning herself with a handkerchief. The policeman was trying to calm her down.

"He nearly knocked me over, the scamp. Never said a word. Took one look at me and skedaddled."

Eric drew up behind the police car.

Alison jumped out. "What happened, Mrs. Duffy?"

"Oh, Miss Alison. Am I relieved to see you! I thought that blackguard was after you."

"What blackguard, Mrs. Duffy?"

"That's what I'd like to know," the officer said. "I'm trying to get a description."

"Let's go inside and talk," Alison suggested.

They followed her into the house.

"A man broke in?" Eric asked the policeman. "And Mrs. Duffy surprised him?"

"So I gather," the officer replied.

"That's what I've been telling him," Mrs. Duffy said. "I came by half an hour ago to return the vacuum cleaner I borrowed from you. I didn't want to wake you—I thought you were at home—so I let myself in with the key. I went to the broom closet and—may the saints preserve me—I see a stranger tripping down the stairs, big as life. Well, I let out a shriek, and he jumps in the air and barrels past me so fast you'd think a banshee's on his tail. Out the door, down the walk, and into a car. Zoom! he's off."

"Was he wearing a suit?" Eric asked.

"A suit?" Mrs. Duffy put a finger to the side of her nose. "Now that I recall, he was."

"What color?"

The effort of recall was reflected in Mrs. Duffy's face. "I think it was light brown. Tan."

"Was his hair flat, Vaseline-slick?" Alison asked.

"Could have been," Mrs. Duffy said.

"Wait a minute, I'm asking the questions," the policeman interjected. "Do you think you know this guy?"

"Just one more question to pin it down, if you don't mind, Officer," Eric said. "What color was his hair?"

"Mind you, I only caught a glimpse of the blackguard," Mrs. Duffy said. "But I'd say it was fair."

"Are you sure it wasn't black?" Eric asked.

"Of course I'm sure. It was sandy."

"Then he's not the guy I was thinking of, Officer. Sorry."

"Who did you have in mind?" the policeman insisted.

"Alison saw a guy loitering around yesterday. But he had black hair, didn't he, Alison?"

"Yes, I'm sure it was black."

"You'd better look around and see if anything was stolen," the policeman suggested. "Money, jewelry. He might have stashed it in his pockets. You can reach me at the station. My name is Perkins."

"Sure thing, Officer, thanks very much," Eric said.

"Oh, by the way, Mrs. Duffy," Perkins asked. "Did you catch the license number?"

"I hardly had time to catch my breath."

"Did you notice if it was an Illinois plate?"

Mrs. Duffy gave him a blank look.

"Can you describe the car?"

"It was a little red car with a foreign name."

"A Volkswagen?"

"Yes, I think that's it."

"Thank you, Mrs. Duffy. If you think of anything else, please let me know."

The policeman got into his car and drove off.

"I'm sorry for all the trouble, Mrs. Duffy," Alison said.

"That's all right, Dear. I hope they catch the thieving rogue. And take my advice: Put a new lock on the door. An expensive one. Time was a man's house was his castle. Today even a castle's not safe—I'll be going along now. Take care of yourselves. If you need anything at all, just call. Mrs. Duffy will be right over."

"Good old Mrs. Duffy," Eric said.

"It could have been the late Mrs. Duffy," Alison added.

"Our friend in the tan suit wouldn't harm her. It's not his style. He's too slick."

"Like his hair," Alison observed.

An idea suddenly dawned on Eric. He leaned over and whispered in Alison's ear, "He might have had time to plant some bugs."

"Not again!"

"You'd better get used to it," Eric whispered. "It comes with the territory. To intelligence agents, security checks are a way of life. Come on, let's reconnoiter."

They spent an hour combing through the house from top to bottom. "No cute little electronic gadgets this time," Alison sighed.

"Nothing missing either," Eric said. "All our important papers are in the study. Untouched, so far as I can tell."

"Mrs. Duffy must have arrived before he got a chance."

Alison felt a sudden pang of guilt about Paul. She'd forgotten to call him. As she reached for the phone, it began to ring, almost telepathically, it seemed.

"Stop! Don't touch it!" Eric cried.

Alison's hand stopped in midair, poised over the receiver. "It might be Paul."

"I know. Don't answer it."

"Do you think the phone is booby trapped?"

"Might be tapped."

Alison squirmed with discomfort as the phone continued to ring. "It's psychologically impossible to ignore a telephone ring. Especially when you know a friend is on the line."

"If they tapped the phone," Eric said, "Paul is the last person we should talk to. He'll spill everything before we have a chance to stop him."

The caller was persistent. But at last the phone stopped ringing.

"I'm no electronic whiz," Eric said, "but I know a tap when I see one." He went to the toolbox and took out a screwdriver. Turning the phone upside down, he removed two restraining screws from the base. The cover slid off, and Eric examined the mechanism.

"Here it is!" he cried triumphantly. His finger indicated a small gadget attached with a clip. "There's your tap. He must've installed it first thing on entering the house."

"No eavesdropper should be without one," Alison cracked.

Eric was about to remove it when Alison stopped him. "No, wait. They want to listen in on our conversations. Let 'em."

"Huh?"

"So long as we don't answer the phone before briefing Paul, there's no problem. He's the only one we can't communicate with over this phone. They mustn't learn we're acquainted. But no one else knows about our caper, and any other phone conversation will be perfectly innocent."

"I see what you mean. We can make the tap work to our own advantage. Let's say one of us phones from an outside line. Knowing they're listening in, we can slip them false leads."

Alison laughed. "We'll make it sound like we're good little Nazis."

"Lay it on real thick—they'll never doubt our loyalty again."

"Unless they begin to suspect we know the phone is tapped," Alison cautioned. "Let's not lay it on so thick that it's obvious."

"But don't be afraid of going overboard on our dedication to Nazi principles."

"Jawohl," Alison said, snapping to attention with a sharp click of her heels.

Eric went to a window and looked out.

"You don't think they still have a tail on us?" Alison asked.

"I don't know." He pulled at his lower lip. "I'd like to phone Paul. But if we're under observation, going out to make a call will look suspicious."

"Let's take a ride to Paul's place," Alison suggested.

"We might as well."

They locked the door, got into the car, and took off.

As they drove, Alison kept glancing through the rear window. "I think we have an escort."

"Blue Datsun?"

"Yes."

Eric turned left, checked the car behind, turned right, rechecked, turned left-right-left, checked again. The Datsun maintained a steady fifty-yard distance.

"They just want to know where we're going," Eric said. "They're not out to hurt us. They've had plenty of opportunities."

"Let's make a run for it," Alison said.

"Glad to oblige." Eric made a sharp turn, whipped through the gears, and rocketed down the street.

Overshooting the mark, the Datsun backed up and swung around the corner as Eric's car shrank into the distance. Eric zigzagged through traffic, coming up short at a red light. Alison fell forward, her head colliding with the dashboard.

"I'm sorry," Eric said. "Are you hurt?"

"No, I always wanted a bump in the center of my forehead. It's a beauty mark in certain cultures."

Eric checked the rearview mirror. The Datsun was rapidly closing the distance. As the light changed, Eric gunned the motor. He turned right, drove through a parking lot and emerged on the other side of the block. The Datsun came speeding straight at them, head-on like a Japanese suicide plane.

Eric swerved, jumped the sidewalk and bucked on up the street, as the Datsun skidded, squealed, rammed a parked car, and tunneled through a brick wall. The sound of the crash resonated like an explosion, with a shower of red-brick dust.

Eric jammed on the brakes.

"Are you all right, Alison?"

"As soon as I get my heart out of my mouth, I'll let you know."

Eric expelled his breath. "I was wrong. He was trying to kill us. The driver's a fanatic."

"I don't think he meant to total us. He got excited and lost control of the car."

"Maybe. But what I can't figure is, if he was just assigned to trail us, why make it so obvious? Why give the game away by chasing the quarry at breakneck speed?"

"These people are totalitarians. They have one-track

minds," Alison said. "Given instructions to follow us, he carried them out to the letter, as he saw them. It's not in their nature to be flexible, to bend with circumstances. They're incapable of compromise."

"We'd better head back and see how he is."

"But we just risked our lives trying to shake him."

"That's when he was all in one piece," Eric said. "He won't be tagging anyone for a long time. You can bet on it."

"Eric, the police will have to make an accident report. We don't want to be officially involved. It might tie us to the Nazis."

"The decision is out of our hands. A police car is pulling up. We can't leave the scene of an accident. We had to jump the curb to avoid him. His car was out of control. There's nothing to link us with him. We don't even know who he is."

"Okay, let's go."

They left the car and walked back to the wreckage. A litter of broken bricks filled the street, and the air was laden with gritty dust. The rear of the Datsun jutted into a small crowd that was beginning to collect. The front end was buried in a landslide of rubble, and two policemen burrowed in the debris for the driver. They had him under the shoulders and began to lift him out. He was unconscious, one side of his face glistening with blood from a gash on the cheek.

"The man in tan!" Alison whispered.

They set him down carefully on the pavement, with people milling about.

"Please stand back! Give him room," one of the policemen urged.

His partner radioed for an ambulance. Then he asked, "Did anyone see what happened?"

A little old bewhiskered man stepped haltingly to the front of the crowd. "I was standing across the street." His voice was barely audible.

"What happened?"

"It crashed into the wall. Real fast like a daredevil. Almost hit that other car." He pointed down the street to Eric's car.

Eric spoke up. "My sister and I were riding in the car. He came charging up a one-way street. I had to jump the sidewalk to avoid him."

The officer turned to the eyewitness. "Is that the way it happened?

"Yes, but I don't want to get involved. I mind my own business."

"There won't be any problem," the policeman assured him. He took the man's name and address, and turning to Eric, said, "He corroborates your story. That lets you off the hook. Nothing to worry about. Do you have insurance?"

Eric nodded.

"Let me see your driver's license and registration."

As they walked back to Eric's car, he introduced himself—"Sergeant Mitchell"—and asked Alison for identification. She showed him her student ID.

"You're both students at Central High?" It was more a statement of fact than a question.

Eric and Alison indicated yes.

"Our father, Randall Thorne, teaches in the School of Agriculture," Eric said. It was gratuitous information, Eric realized, offered out of anxiety.

"Did you ever see the driver before?" Mitchell asked.

Alison bit her lip and hesitated. Officer Mitchell observed her carefully. She was obviously struggling with how she should respond.

The policeman sensed something. "You sure you haven't seen the driver before?" Years on the force had taught him to "smell" when someone was holding back.

"I think I've seen him somewhere," Alison responded with honesty, "but I have no idea who he is."

"How about you?" The officer was studying Eric's face.

"I don't know who he is, either." Eric answered in a firm voice that left no room for qualification.

"We have to follow up all possibilities, you understand," Mitchell said. "He doesn't carry any identification."

An ambulance drew up at the curb. Two attendants got out and examined the man. "Possible concussion," one of them said. They lifted him gently onto a stretcher and loaded it in the back of the ambulance. One of the attendants got in the driver's seat, switched on the siren, and pulled out.

"Will you let us know his condition, Officer?" Eric asked.

"We'll be in touch. You're not leaving town in the next few days, are you?"

"No, not that I know of." Eric grimaced slightly.

Officer Mitchell gave Eric a curious look, put his pad away deliberately, and stepped into the patrol car, his forehead creased in a thoughtful frown.

# 11 • Fooled

Eric turned the car around and headed for Paul's house.

"I'm afraid Sergeant Mitchell suspects something," Alison said.

"He's searching for a motive, but has nothing to go on. That's frustrating."

"Yes, he is obviously dissatisfied. He thinks we're holding back something."

"He'll track the license plate, which probably is stolen. At the moment, that's his only lead."

"What happens when 'tan suit' revives?" Alison asked.

"With that bash in his skull, he'll probably have amnesia."

"Don't count on it."

"But he could easily simulate amnesia. It's the logical way out for a secret operator. It's what I'd do in his place."

"James Bond Thorne."

"In any case, 'tan suit' won't give them anything; you can be sure of that."

"I'm wondering what his Nazi pals will make of it," Alison said.

"No problem there. If they ask us, we'll say we tried to give him the slip, not knowing who was tagging us. It might have been the FBI."

"They'll probably figure we got scared. 'Tan suit' bungled it. They'll put him down as an incompetent." Alison giggled. "Can't even tail two high school kids without getting caught."

They drove up Hobart Lane to an intersection which brought them within view of University Hospital.

Eric rubbed his chin. "I don't know. Officer Mitchell said he'd let us know his condition. But I guess it would be the right thing to do."

"It won't take long," Alison said.

"Okay, let's go."

Eric pulled around to the Emergency Entrance and parked across the street.

They passed a security guard who looked them over, but made no effort to stop them. People wandered in and out of Emergency all day long.

Eric recalled the last time they were in the hospital. They were children. Eric had a case of infected tonsils, and the surgeon suggested removing Alison's tonsils at the same time.

The smell of hospital antiseptic drifted along the corridor. Visitors sat in clusters, faces drawn, tense, apprehensive. An orderly wheeled a patient into an elevator.

"It's not our man," Eric whispered.

A staff physician, dressed in surgical green, spoke rapidly to a nurse, then dashed into the elevator as the doors slid shut.

Eric and Alison walked over to the admission desk. A nurse glanced at them impassively. She was a big boned woman with plain features and wispy hair. "Yes?" she asked.

"We'd like to know the condition of an accident victim," Alison said.

"The patient's name?"

"We don't know," Alison said. "He was wearing a tan suit. Had a gash in the side of his face. About thirty years old."

"When did the accident take place?"

"I've been on duty for two hours. I don't recall anything about an accident victim with a head injury. Are you sure he was brought here?"

"Quite sure," Eric said.

"Let me double check the records." She riffled through a stack of papers. "Can you describe the man again, please?"

"Thin, medium built, brown hair parted in the center, combed flat, wearing a tan suit," Eric said.

"That doesn't ring any bells with me. Are you sure he was admitted to this hospital?"

There were only two hospitals in Ivy. The other one was located at the far end of town.

"The accident wasn't far from here," Alison said. "Aren't crash victims normally treated here?"

"Normally, yes. Did you see the man put into an ambulance?"

"Yes."

"Was there a police report?"

"Yes, two policemen were on the scene. They must have radioed for the ambulance."

"That's strange. Hold on, I'll phone Newport Hospital."

"Thank you," Alison said.

The nurse phoned the hospital, relayed the patient's description and the nature of the accident. She held the line for a minute, then put down the phone, perplexed. "They say there has been no patient answering that description. And no auto victim from this vicinity."

"He must be here," Eric insisted. "Maybe he hasn't been officially admitted yet. Can we look in those little emergency rooms?"

The nurse gave a shrug of impatience. "Only hospital personnel are allowed in first-aid rooms. I assure you, any patient who enters the hospital is automatically tagged; a chart is prepared and the intern enters his observations. I write up every emergency patient; and there has been no auto victim within the past two hours." The matter was closed. She turned to a man approaching the desk. "May I help you?"

Eric and Alison walked toward the exit. The security guard stared at them without interest.

"We're trying to locate a man who came in an ambulance about forty-five minutes ago," Eric said.

"Brown hair plastered down, unconscious, a cut on the right cheek," Alison added.

The guard shook his head. "He didn't come through here."

"How long have you been on duty?"

94

"Two hours. Did you ask the desk nurse?"

"Yes. Thank you," Alison said.

They went outside.

"What do you make of it?" Eric asked.

"Either there's a cover-up at the hospitals, or our friend never made it here."

"I think we can rule out the first possibility. Why would they conceal his admission? Aside from the fact that it's illegal, it would be almost impossible to cover an emergency so soon in a hospital this size. Too many witnesses; too many papers to falsify."

"I wasn't suggesting that's what happened," Alison said. "Something must have happened to him on the way to the hospital."

"Let's say the ambulance he was in had an accident," Eric proposed.

"I don't think that's likely. It's only a few blocks from here that the ambulance picked him up," Alison commented.

Eric wrinkled his forehead. "That leaves one real possibility," he said slowly.

"Are you thinking what I'm thinking?" Alison flashed.

"Yeah! It was a phony ambulance!"

"Probably sent by Phoenix, and the two paramedics were Nazis. They were afraid 'tan suit' might talk when he came to, or make a slip. So they picked him up."

"They must have intercepted the accident report on the police band," Alison said. "They knew it was their man from the description of the car and the license number. But they had to have some way of diverting the hospital ambulance and substituting their own."

"Through somebody on the police force who could cancel the hospital call."

"It wouldn't necessarily be the police," Alison suggested. "The police department has a lot of clerical help. It could have been one of the ambulance dispatchers."

"However the Nazis worked it, they're the most likely culprits. 'Tan suit' didn't just vanish into thin air."

"He's probably already back in Millbrook," Alison said.

"Wait till Sergeant Mitchell hears about this! If he was suspicious before—"

"If they ran it back to Millbrook, someone had to see it."

Eric had a sudden hunch. "You know where the ambulance is? It's probably locked in a garage somewhere in Ivy."

"I think you're right. And the Nazis have the key."

"We could search for it," Eric said.

"If you're good at finding needles in haystacks. Do you have any idea how many garages there are in Ivy?"

"In the process, we'd probably get arrested for breaking and entry."

"And Mitchell would be the arresting officer!" Alison said.

They got in the car and continued across town. Alison kept watching to see if they were followed. It had become second nature.

She wondered how many Nazis lived in Ivy. It would be to their advantage to infiltrate the community, to gain sympathizers and even recruits from among student activists. According to Paul's anonymous informant, one of Midwest's professors was a closet Nazi. Were there any other faculty members with Nazi sympathies? It seemed hard to believe, but—

Eric broke into Alison's thoughts. "Paul didn't mention anything about a burglary at his house, did he?"

"No, why?"

"I just wondered."

"If we're not careful, we'll soon be as paranoid as they are," Alison said.

They were approaching Paul's block. Eric's antennae were working as well as Alison's. He turned slowly up the street, inspecting parked cars for occupants. They were all empty. It was unlikely that Paul would be under surveillance. The Nazis were confident they had scared him into inaction. As a precaution, however, Eric parked two blocks away and phoned Paul from a corner booth.

"Hello," Paul's voice was ragged.

Before answering, Eric listened for any suspicious clicks on the line.

"Hello?" Paul repeated.

Still no clicks. They should come at twenty-second intervals.

"HELLO!" Paul shouted.

The line sounded clear. This wasn't a foolproof indication, but it was probably safe to talk.

"Paul, this is Eric."

"Eric! You got away. Great!"

"I'll tell you all about it later, Paul."

"Where are you calling from?"

"A few blocks away."

"Why don't you come over? Are you being tailed?"

"We were before, by a car. The driver had an accident."

"You think someone is watching my place? Is that it?"

"I don't see anyone, but to play it safe, meet us at the corner of Maple and Grove. We'll be sitting in the car. From our location, we can see whether anyone follows you."

"Okay, I'm leaving now," Paul said.

Eric took a bead on Paul's house. He had an unobstructed line of vision.

"You check the right-hand side of the street. I'll check the left," Eric suggested.

Alison nodded.

They watched Paul leave the house and proceed east on Maple.

Five seconds later, Alison said, "There's a man coming out of a basement across from Paul."

Eric followed her gaze to a house on the opposite corner. "I see him. Did Paul notice him?"

"I don't think so. He wasn't looking in that direction. He's a burly-looking man in T-shirt and jeans, about six feet tall. Carries himself like a weight lifter."

Paul paused on the next corner, waiting for the light to change. The man crossed to the other side of the street. He was still outside Paul's field of vision. Walking deliberately, he came within sixty feet of Paul.

Paul continued up the street. He was a block away now. He gazed straight ahead, without glancing over his shoulder. The man maintained a constant distance between them. Eric saw that he was wearing sneakers.

"Look around, Paul!" Eric pleaded. It was impossible to signal him without giving away their presence to the man behind him.

As Paul came up alongside the car, Eric made an inconspicuous gesture that was meant to say, "Keep walking." But Paul didn't give him a glance. Staring straight ahead, he continued walking past the car. He had seen the man, after all!

Eric and Alison ducked under the seat as the man approached. They mustn't be seen in the vicinity. They hoped the man was unfamiliar with their car.

Paul turned the next corner. The first test. Walking at the same measured pace, the man approached the corner and turned in the same direction.

"I'm going after them!" Eric said, reaching for the door handle.

Alison grabbed his wrist. "You can't. It'll give us away. So far, there's nothing to connect us with Paul."

"I can't stop to argue with you, Alison." He wrenched open the door on his side.

"But he's not out to hurt Paul. He was just assigned to tail him."

"Do you know that for a fact?"

"Why else would he be following him? If you go out now, you'll just be playing into their hands. And what will you accomplish? Nothing."

Eric sat poised on the edge of his seat, seething, his body coiled for action, waging a battle with himself. Then, suddenly deflated, he sank back with a defeated expression. "I guess you're right. I wasn't thinking."

"Paul can handle himself," Alison said, as much to reassure herself as Eric.

They sat in the car without speaking. Inaction took an act of will on Eric's part. A friend was in trouble. Eric's instinct was to abandon caution. But Alison was right. He would risk everything in one rash act of derring-do. Only the Nazis could benefit.

But doing nothing—that was almost impossible.

A long ten minutes passed, and a cheerful whistle floated down the street. Paul came strolling around the corner, looking like the cat that swallowed the rat. He strutted up to the car.

"Fancy meeting you here," he said.

"Paul, what happened?" Alison exclaimed.

"Did you shake him?" Eric asked.

"No need to. I just put him under a magic spell, said 'abracadabra,' and poof! he disappeared. Just like Blackstone the Magician. Blackstone didn't perform in black face, did he?"

"Only in minstrel shows," Eric quipped. "Where did you accomplish this feat?"

"About two blocks down the Grove. The guy turned up Merrick Road and went on his merry way."

"He wasn't following you, after all," Alison said.

"A brilliant deduction," Eric gibed.

"Following me? I followed him for half a block. He ended up at the Y!"

# 12 • Threatened

Paul got into the car beside Eric and Alison.

He turned to Eric. "Did Alison tell you about her call last evening?"

"Yes, she did."

"You really gave me a scare, Alison. I was up all night worrying. When did you get back, Eric?"

"Last night."

"Last night! Why didn't you phone me? Alison promised."

"She wanted to," Eric said, "but we were afraid we were being watched. We couldn't go out to phone; it would have looked suspicious. And it wasn't safe to use the motel phone."

"I understand," Paul said. "I should have thought of that. But when I didn't hear from Alison, I assumed the worst. What did happen to you?"

Eric related his meeting with Fred Purdon, the trip to the warehouse, and his grilling by the bogus Nazi generals. On his return to the motel, he learned that their rooms had been cased. In the morning when they returned to Ivy, they found their house phone tapped.

Alison went on to describe the car chase and the case of the missing man in tan.

"Wow!" Paul blew out his breath. "You two have been busy. Those weirdo generals give me the willies. That was a close scrape you had."

"Closer than a Gillette Trac II razor." Eric rubbed his throat.

"What do you think their next move will be?"

"They said they'd contact me in a few days. This gives them time to check out my background."

"Time to discover the Earl story is phony."

"They already suspect that. But as professional liars, practiced in the art of deception, they're prepared to overlook a lie, provided I seem the right sort of person. They believe I have personal reasons for concealing my source, the guy who really tipped me to Phoenix. Goebbels thinks I'm too incompetent to be a spy! Why would the FBI recruit a clown like me?"

"He has a point," Paul said with an explosive laugh. Then sobering, "But you have to win their trust. You've probably got one strike against you."

"Two strikes if Goering calls the shots."

"Maybe it's time to cut out altogether. While you still have your health. All three of us can take our case to the FBI."

"Just when things are getting interesting?" Eric protested. "Not on your life."

"We went over this last night," Alison said. "We don't have any hard evidence. We don't know who the

Halloween generals are, or where their headquarters is located. The man in tan disappeared; so we can't get anything out of him. We can't corroborate a thing."

"We wouldn't even make credible witnesses in a court of law," Eric said. "Not at this stage of our investigation."

"But why would we concoct such a story?" Paul asked.

"They might think it's a prank!" Eric said. "A dare. Or we're doing it for kicks."

Paul spread his hands in resignation. "You're probably right," he conceded. "But I still wish you wouldn't mess with those Nazi cats any more."

"As long as we remain one step ahead of them, we'll be okay," Eric said. "We started this, we've got to see it through. If we give up now, they've won."

"With any luck, we will ferret out the whole gang of them," Alison said.

"I won't be any help to you, stuck here in Ivy," Paul said. "You will keep in touch?"

"Of course," Alison said.

"I can't even phone your home," Paul said. "So long as it's tapped."

"I know. I'm sorry," Eric said. "But it's for a good cause. Alison and I intend to rig a conversation glowing with Nazi fervor."

Paul gave a chuckle of amusement. "Give them a good earful."

He opened the door on his side. As he got out, he said, "As my nautical Irish ancestors used to say, 'May yer have clear sailing and a fair wind at yer back.'"

"Well put, me hearty," Eric said. "See you later."

He turned the ignition key. As the car made off, Paul called, "Good luck!"

They drove home, had a light lunch, then followed their separate pursuits. Alison wound up the metronome and did her Czerny piano exercises, while Eric cracked some books.

"I'll get it," Eric yelled when the phone rang a while later.

"Eric, don't forget: the phone has a third ear," she called up the stairs.

"I won't," Eric said, picking up the receiver. "Hello."

"Is this the Thorne residence?"

"Yes."

"May I speak to Eric Thorne, please?"

"Speaking."

"This is Miss Atkins. I'm calling from the Administration Office of Central High School. I thought I should let you know about some calls we've received."

"About me?" Eric asked.

"Yes. Three callers requested confidential information about you and your family. We told them they would have to submit the appropriate forms, copies of which we would forward to the student for his approval, before divulging any information. But they're very persistent and keep phoning. Perhaps they don't understand English well; two of them sound like foreigners."

"Did they identify themselves?"

"They say they're prospective employers. If you have any idea who they are, you might get in touch with them. We're only allowed to release information to government agencies, and to private parties who submit the appropriate form."

"Thank you, Miss Atkins. I appreciate your bringing this to my attention."

He replaced the phone in its cradle.

"What was that all about?" Alison asked.

"The Nazis have been calling Central High requesting personal data about me. Administration refused to give it without my consent."

"You should have told her that if a Mr. Goebbels, Goering, Himmler, or Heydrich calls, it's all right to divulge our kinship to Adolf Eichmann."

"If that's their idea of checking me out, they're a bunch of turkeys," Eric said.

He flopped down on the sofa with a book standing open on his chest. Gradually his eyelids grew heavy, fluttered, and closed, the book sliding noiselessly to the carpeted floor.

He was slipping off the edge of a precipice. At the bottom stood a wolfhound, its great haunches braced to leap at his throat.

Eric woke with a start, his body cramped into a corkscrew position, knees dangling halfway over the sofa. The hazy light of dusk slanted through the windows. He rubbed his eyes, squinting at the luminous hands of his watch. Five-forty. He must have slept for hours.

He felt uneasy. Something had wakened him. A scuffling sound. Or was it the trailing echo of his dream: the wolfhound rearing up, straining impatiently, hind legs kicking up sand.

The doorbell rang.

"Who is it?" Eric called.

"Hurry please, open the door!" a high-pitched male voice pleaded. There was a banging of fists on the door.

Impulsively, Eric ran to the door and threw it open. There stood a small, inoffensive-looking man wearing thick bifocals. For some reason, he was cringing on the doorstep. A leather briefcase was jammed under one arm.

Eric heard a car rev up down the street. The effect on the little man was electric. He stood as though glued against the wall, shivering and pointing at a black car rapidly approaching. The car was upon them within seconds after Eric opened the door. The rear near-side window was rolled down. Eric saw a cylindrical object jutting out. It was too late to run. Eric threw himself to the floor of the porch. The silencer pumped twice with a muffled discharge.

The first bullet hit the man in the shoulder and pinned him to the wall. The second bit off a chunk of concrete that whanged against the garden wall.

Eric heard the diminishing sound of the car trailing off down the street. He got to his feet as the small man crumpled, falling forward into his arms.

"Take the briefcase! Hurry!" he gasped. "Take it to Phoenix." Thrusting the briefcase into Eric's hands, the man lurched toward the street.

"Let me help you," Eric said, reaching out. "Come inside."

"Let me alone!" His thin voice was rattled. His face was twisted with pain. He reeled down the steps of the porch toward the street, arms outthrust like a drunken dervish, uncannily managing to keep erect. "Don't open the briefcase," he warned. In the next instant he was lost in the shadows.

Eric's eyes strained into the deepening dusk. He was gone. There was not a trace of him, not even a drop of blood on the pavement.

An idea ricochcted through Eric's brain like a bullet. The scene was almost too theatrical. Staged. Staged by Phoenix to test his reliability. The question they posed: would he turn the briefcase over to them?

Eric exploded with laughter. He tossed the briefcase high in the air, catching it on the downswing. They had him going for a while, but he had seen through their flimsy charade.

Twirling the briefcase in is hand, he turned to go into the house.

Alison was standing in the doorway, eyes wide, eyebrows arched in puzzlement. "Did I miss something? I was in the shower when the bell rang."

"Not much," Eric said, ushering Alison into the house. "A guy from Phoenix took a slug in the chest from a hit car, gave me this briefcase to deliver, and stumbled off down the street."

"Oh, is that all? Did anyone tell you you have a morbid sense of humor?"

"I'm not kidding. That's exactly what happened. It was a put-on staged for our benefit. Very convincing. Only the guy didn't bleed when he was shot! They forgot the tomato ketchup."

Alison listened patiently. "Number one, I didn't see anyone when I came down. Number two, I didn't hear a shot."

"Number three, I have the briefcase in my hand. Alison, I haven't lost my marbles."

Alison made him go over the whole story from beginning to end. When he was finished, she inspected the nick in the wall where the concrete broke off.

"No blank did that," she observed.

"No, that was a real bullet. The slug the guy took was a dud."

Alison examined the entrance for signs of blood. Not a drop. "Amateurs," she said with disgust.

Eric stowed the briefcase in his room, then showered, while Alison whipped up something to eat. She was putting out the dishes when the doorbell rang. Eric and Alison sprang to cautious attention.

This time Eric looked through the peephole before opening the door.

There stood a well-groomed, conservatively dressed man with sharply inquisitive eyes and a rugged jawline. Eric guessed he was about forty.

Cautiously, Eric opened a crack in the door.

"FBI." Then he reached into his coat and produced a badge. "I'm Inspector Nelson. I'd like to talk to you."

"Come in. We can talk in here."

The inspector followed Eric into the living room.

"I'm Eric Thorne. This is my sister Alison."

"How do you do?"

"Have a seat."

"Thanks. Without further preliminaries, I want to compliment you on your investigation of Phoenix."

"Phoenix? Phoenix, Arizona? I've never been in Arizona," Eric said.

108

Nelson chuckled dryly, without amusement. "You can drop the act. We've been onto you from the beginning. We followed your movements in Millbrook."

"I don't mean to sound rude, Inspector, but would you mind telling me what you're talking about?"

"Look, kid, let down your hair. You're with a friend. I admire the initiative you and your sister here have shown."

"You must have us confused with someone else," Eric said.

Nelson looked sharply at Eric. "Didn't you meet with Fred Purdon in Millbrook?"

"The guy in the cafe? His name was Fred something-or-other. It might have been Purdon."

"And didn't you accompany him in his car?"

"We went for a hop. Do you mind telling me what this is all about?"

"You're making a mistake, playing dumb. You're tangled up with a vicious bunch, and you're endangering your sister's life as well as your own. Let me give you some advice. Don't go it on your own. You don't know what you're getting into."

"Inspector, we appreciate your concern," Eric said. "But I'm afraid somebody sent you out here on a wild goose chase."

Nelson's jaw tightened. He rose to his feet. "Look, I could take you both down to the Bureau. But I won't. I will have to report this conversation. It will go into the FBI files and follow you the rest of your lives. One more thing—before I leave, hand over the briefcase."

"Briefcase? What briefcase?"

"You want me to return with a search warrant?"

"I think you'd better leave. I don't even own a brief-case," Eric said.

"We found Muller down the street. Stone-dead. Before he died, he ditched the briefcase, and we know you have it. You may not be aware of the contents. I have to warn you. If you withhold it, you may be tried for treason."

"I don't know anyone named Muller. Do you, Alison?"

"No."

"That's your final word?"

"Yes. Sorry we can't help you," Eric said.

"I'll be back," Nelson said. "Don't bother showing me out." He strode to the door, twisted the knob, and pulled it open.

The door closed with a jar.

# 13 • Death Leap

"That's the last we'll see of Nelson," Alison said.

"You're real sharp, Alison. I was afraid you'd spill the beans. How did you catch on so fast?"

"That he was a Nazi? Elementary. FBI agents don't bow to the waist when introduced to a lady."

"Smart gal! That was Part One of the Phoenix test. To see whether we're FBI operatives or willing to cooperate with the FBI. We passed that test. Now comes Part Two."

"To see whether we surrender the briefcase under pressure."

"Exactly," Eric said. "We're supposed to believe that Nelson is going to return with a search squad. The inference is that one of Nelson's men is posted outside to prevent us from getting it off our hands.

"If we refuse to bow to pressure, and retain the briefcase, Phoenix wants to see how resourceful we are in getting it to them."

111

"That leaves us with two choices," Eric said. "Either we find an undetectable hiding place or we remove it from the house."

"The first is out," Alison said. "Underestimating the FBI's ability to find the briefcase would be dumb. There is no secure hiding place in the house. The FBI would take the place apart, if need be. But they'd find it."

"So we're left with the second choice. Problem: How do we sneak it out with an agent posted outside?"

"We could leave the house in different directions, carrying identical parcels."

"That's too simple. The agent pulls a gun and orders us both to halt. Or he might have a partner, one to tail each of us. There might be two men outside."

"If there are two of them," Alison said, "we have to assume one is covering the back door."

"Okay, let's make that assumption. Both exits are blocked, and one of us has to get out of the house. Could we create a diversion that would pull the man in the back around to the front?"

Alison's eyes narrowed reflectively. "Something dramatic, some emergency perhaps. Something important enough to make him leave his post."

They were silent for a space, turning the problem over in their minds. Eric made the first suggestion. "Suppose we phone for a private ambulance. The sound of a siren—followed by the ambulance pulling up at the house—will draw him away from the back."

"Not if they're in two-way communication. Agents carry walkie-talkies. They won't fall for it. The guy in the back will stay there, as directed, unless his partner fails to respond."

"So how do you jam a walkie-talkie?" Eric asked.

"Don't ask me."

Eric's features contracted in thought. "You'd need a signal generator to overpower the frequency they're operating on. Naturally, we don't have one."

"So much for that."

"Okay, if we rule out a diversion, the only thing that's left is the roof," Eric said.

"The roof?"

"Crossing over from our roof to the Mercers' house."

"You mean leaping across?" Alison exclaimed. "There's a seven-foot gulf between the Mercers' house and ours. Did you ever try jumping seven feet from a standing start?"

"Not across empty space. But it can be done."

"Maybe it can—by a track star. Remember the roof is tilted. You wouldn't even be able to get a running start. You could break your neck!"

"Ever since I was a kid, I've wanted to jump across to the other roof. Stop worrying so much."

"If you're really serious about it, at least put on your sneakers. They'll give you more traction."

"Yes, Mother—now—enough conversation. Let's get the ball rolling."

Eric went upstairs, laced on his sneakers, and slipped on a dark sweater. Then he sealed the briefcase in wrapping paper. Alison suggested a diversion to occupy one of the men while Eric made his leap. By this time, they were convinced that two men were stationed outside. Alison decided to leave the house with a shopping bag. The man in front, posing as an FBI agent, would stop her to examine its contents.

"When I hear you leave the house, that will be my cue to jump," Eric said.

"Don't yell 'Geronimo!' " Alison said.

"And don't forget to leave the lights on. Turn up the stereo before you go. We have to make it look as if I'm still home."

Alison filled a shopping bag with library books. When the fictitious agent stopped her, she would explain that she was returning the books to the library. If he asked about Eric, she would say he was spending the evening at home.

Alison accompanied Eric to the attic and watched him mount the ladder to the roof. Except for a thin stream of moonlight, the room was sunk in darkness. Even a candle's glow might attract attention to the attic.

Eric felt his way up the ladder, step by step, the packaged briefcase tucked under one arm. At the top, he raised the trapdoor, just behind the chimney, leading to the roof and climbed out.

Crawling on hands and knees, he inched across to the side of the house opposite their neighbor's. The distance between the houses seemed wider than he remembered. An inky void stretched before him, with a concrete floor at least thirty feet below.

If only he had more time to prepare for the jump. Normally, he would limber up with stretching exercises. But if he stood erect, his silhouette would stand out against the moon. Once he made his move to a standing position, he'd have only seconds to execute the leap.

He rose to an awkward crouch, resting his weight on his fists. The air was cool, the wind brisk. But his forehead streamed with perspiration. He wiped it off with his sleeve. He could feel his palms slippery.

He tried to recall the last time he performed a standing jump. It was back in high school, as a sophomore. He spanned seven feet handily. But conditions were different. He landed in a sandbox; the impact cushioned—not across seven feet of empty space.

He heard Alison close the front door. Without a moment's hesitation, he sprang up and reared back to jump—but his legs were locked in place. He stood on the edge of the roof, stiff-legged and irresolute. Jump! he commanded his legs—they wouldn't obey. Jump, now! Perspiration saturated his shirt. His eyes measured the distance to the ground below, and for one unnerving moment his head reeled. He was afraid of losing his balance and toppling forward. He stepped back from the edge, tension drying his throat.

A man's voice called out below. But it wasn't directed at him. He heard Alison respond, and caught snatches of their conversation.

"I'll have to look in that bag, Miss."

"It's only books. I'm on my way to the library."

Alison was stalling for time, giving him ample opportunity to make the jump and get away.

Make the jump!

He could hear his heart pounding. He had to throw off this nightmare paralysis. But was it worth the risk? All this cloak-and-dagger stuff certainly wasn't worth his life. But if he gave up now, the Nazis would win. He kept telling himself that over and over. He became angry, angry at himself and angry at the Nazis for placing him in this situation. They were playing him like a puppet, pulling the strings, and waiting to see how he responded. But their advantage was temporary, and in the end he would beat them at their own game. He was determined to beat them. He could feel the adrenaline begin to flow, pumping him up with energy and excitement. Inching forward, he braced his legs and catapulted into space.

He hit the other roof with a jar that sent him sprawling on his knees. But he had a one-foot clearance from the edge, and he was able to rest, panting, savoring the exultation of surviving what might have been a death leap.

"Thank you, Lord!" he gasped.

There were footsteps in the alley below. Eric peered over the edge. A man was circling the back of the house, combing the shrubbery. He shot a look up at the roof. Eric dipped his head, and his body pancaked against the roof.

He heard Mrs. Mercer's voice through a partly open window. She was saying something about the roof, insisting she heard a crash. The antenna might have fallen. Mr. Mercer reluctantly agreed to go up and take a look. Eric doubted that his presence would be welcome on the Mercers' roof.

He sprang up, his sneakers beating a soft tattoo across the shingles. He crossed to the opposite side, located a water pipe, and slid to the ground. The Mercers' high picket fence concealed him from his own backyard. He crawled through a hedge into the next yard and hopped a fence. A dog began to bark. A window shot open. Eric ducked into the shadows, flattening himself against a wall. Sneaking past the Cliftons' house, he continued

116

creeping soundlessly until he reached the last house on the block.

He came out on a side street running perpendicular to Campus Avenue. He glanced along the length of the street. It appeared to be empty. Brushing off his clothes, he proceeded north, turning right on the next corner. It was a mile walk to the railroad depot. Walking briskly, he covered the distance in ten minutes.

A train was pulling in, and a dozen or so people were scattered along the platform. Eric entered the terminal and checked the parcel in a locker. The briefcase was finally off his hands, but now he held the key to the locker. He had to get rid of it. If one of Phoenix's men, still posing as an FBI agent, searched him when he got back, it would be found and give away the briefcase's location. The whole exercise would end in failure.

Eric went into a drug store and bought a box of stationery. He placed the key inside an envelope and addressed it to himself. Then he got some stamps from a vending machine. In large letters, he wrote the words, "special delivery" across the envelope. He licked the stamps and attached them to the letter. Then dropped the envelope in a mailbox and started home.

On his way home, he stopped in another drug store to make a call. Alison was probably back by now. Eric decided it was time to put the phone tap to good use. He dialed his number. Alison answered.

"Hello, Alison. This is Eric. I disposed of the briefcase."

That should shake the Nazis up! So far as they knew, he was still at home. He heard a telltale click on the line; they were listening in. He hoped they got a good earful.

"How did you make it past Nelson's men? They're watching both exits."

"It was easy. I'll tell you all about it later. They're not very bright." Eric heard Alison suppress a giggle. "The main thing is, the briefcase is in a safe place. The FBI won't get their hands on it."

"That's great. Whatever its contents, I hope it makes a contribution to Phoenix."

"Maybe now they'll believe in the sincerity of our commitment to the cause."

"They can't be too cautious about admitting new members," Alison said. "As they get to know us, they'll develop more trust."

"I'm sure they'll never find two more loyal disciples."

"Where are you now?" Alison asked.

"I'm on my way home. Heil Hitler!"

"Heil Hitler!"

Eric hung up, suppressed his laughter, and nodded to the proprietor of the store on his way out.

When he arrived home, he was stopped outside by an official-looking man who flashed an FBI badge.

"I'm Special Agent Lambert, one of Inspector Nelson's men. I'll have to frisk you."

"Are you looking for anything in particular? Maybe I can save you the trouble."

The man ignored his remark. "We'd better step inside the house."

Eric unlocked the door. Alison was standing in the entrance.

"This gentleman is from the FBI," Eric said.

"We've met," Alison answered.

"He wants to frisk me."

"Would you mind leaving the room, Miss? Your brother will have to undress."

Lambert (as he referred to himself) turned Eric's pockets inside out, carefully inspecting the contents. Then he asked Eric to remove his shoes and socks. After examining them, he told Eric to remove the rest of his clothes.

As Eric undressed, Lambert said, "That was a neat stunt you pulled, going over the roof."

"When did you catch on?"

"Not soon enough."

Lambert inspected Eric's clothes thoroughly, inch by inch. He did not mention the object of his search, but Eric knew. They had guessed correctly that Eric checked the briefcase in a locker. Now they wanted to see whether he was sharp enough to dispose of the key before returning home.

After satisfying himself that the key was not secreted on Eric's person, Lambert told Eric to get dressed. "That will be all."

"You're not going to book me?" Eric asked with mock surprise.

"That will depend on Inspector Nelson," he answered shortly and turned to leave.

"Good night," Eric said, as he closed the door behind Lambert.

# 14 • The Fuhrer

The call from Phoenix came the following afternoon. Fred Purdon was on the phone.

"How's it going, kid?"

"Pretty good," Eric answered.

"Did you locate that Earl fellow?"

Eric winced. Earl again!

"I haven't had a chance. I was occupied with other matters. The FBI were breathing down my neck."

"How so?"

"Muller left a briefcase with instructions to deliver it to Phoenix. Soon after, an FBI agent named Nelson called at the house. He knew about the briefcase and pressured me to surrender it. Naturally I didn't."

"Did he case the house?"

"He threatened to, but never did."

"Where's the briefcase now?"

"I managed to sneak it out of the house, and checked it in a locker at the railroad depot."

"Good work. Do you have the key?"

"It's on me now."

There was a slight pause. Eric pictured Purdon trying to figure out how he sneaked the key past Lambert. The self-addressed envelope containing the key had arrived that morning.

"All right, hold on to it. I have good news for you, kid. You passed the initial screening. The rest is up to you. You'll be judged on your future performance."

"I'm happy to hear it."

"The Fuhrer is giving a talk Monday evening. Can you make it?"

"Of course."

"Meet me in the lobby of the Inn Town Motel at seven-thirty sharp. From there I'll take you to the lecture hall."

"Sure thing. I'm looking forward to it."

Purdon said good-bye and hung up.

Eric arrived in Millbrook fifteen minutes early, and decided to stretch his legs a bit. He parked the car a few blocks from the motel. As he passed people on the street, he sensed an aura of expectation. He couldn't tell whether the prevailing feeling was negative or positive; but something was definitely in the air.

As he entered the motel, the desk clerk's frosty glance was a few degrees warmer. *Purdon must have tipped him to my new status,* Eric thought.

Purdon was sitting in a lounge chair, legs crossed, an open Coke bottle in his hand.

"This is for you, kid," he said, as Eric approached him. He gave a hyena cackle.

"Thanks," Eric said.

Reaching inside his coat pocket, Purdon withdrew a flask. "For old times' sake," he said, taking a swig. Then he stood up and walked toward the entrance, with Eric at his side.

They got into Purdon's car. As he started the engine, Purdon said, "You can give me the key to the locker now."

Eric handed it to him. He took it nonchalantly, with no particular interest. Muller's briefcase was probably stuffed with newspapers.

"We expect a full house tonight. The auditorium seats about three hundred."

"I'm eager to see the Fuhrer," Eric said, "I really know very little about him."

"Hasn't anyone briefed you?"

"You're the only member I've spoken to, apart from the generals."

"The generals! That's a hot one!" When his merriment subsided, he began to speak about the Fuhrer in tones of reverence and awe. His name was Werner Kleist. He had been one of Hitler's star pupils in the Nazi youth movement. While too young to serve in the army, he had completely identified with Hitler as Germany's self-proclaimed messiah. He yearned to see the fatherland regain its position as a world power, and echoed Hitler's furious indignation at Germany's humiliation following World War I.

When Hitler died, Kleist's sorrow was so deep and inconsolable that he had to be hospitalized for acute depression. Life lost its meaning for him when Hitler had discharged a bullet into his own skull. But Kleist was young and, in time, began to reassemble the pieces of his life. After World War II, he found his way to the United States, and slowly built a following as a mystical, right-wing fanatic.

Purdon pulled up in front of a square brick building housing a medium-sized auditorium. People were milling about the entrance, buzzing in tones of delighted awe about the speaker.

Most of the seats were already taken. The first row was completely occupied by men in khaki jackets. Kleist's bodyguards and bully boys, Eric surmised. About a third of the audience consisted of women. Eric and Purdon took seats on the right side of the hall.

A striking red banner marked with a black swastika served as a backdrop. Suspended from the ceiling, a large poster of Adolf Hilter gazed down upon the multitude.

Music suddenly blared from two overhead speakers. It broke in waves over the audience like ocean combers flattening a beach—loud martial music with shrill brass fanfares and sustained drum rolls. A cortege of men entered from the wings, marching out upon the stage with an exaggerated military bearing. Their faces were the faces of the generals who had interrogated Eric. They were joined by other men wearing masks of highly placed Nazis—Martin Bormann, Erwin Rommel, Adolf Eichmann. Eric couldn't identify all of the faces. They arranged themselves around the dais—the Fuhrer's honor guard, no doubt.

The music stopped abruptly, and an expectant murmur arose. Then people were on their feet, clapping wildly as the speaker walked out on stage. Kleist was a man of medium stature with a tight, hard appearance that bore an uncanny resemblance to Hitler. The resemblance, Eric decided, was not so much in his features as in his presence and mannerisms. He had thick dark hair flecked with gray, an abbreviated mustache, and small suspicious eyes. There was nothing majestic or magnetic about him. He was not the sort of person who would stand out in a crowd. But when he spoke, his voice was penetrating and loud enough to fill the hall without a microphone. It was the trained voice of a professional speaker or pitchman: aggressive, confident, manipulative—a voice that demanded attention.

"I thank you for your gracious reception," he said. "You will not see any parlor tricks performed here. If you came in with the mistaken impression that I would regale you with mystifying, eye-popping stunts, you are advised to leave now." He looked around the audience. No one moved.

"You are probably aware that I am a psychic, a mentalist in touch with the spirit world. I am not a quack who makes tables rise or spikes bend. You will, indeed, see some astounding things before you leave tonight. These are not feats of magic, but spirit manifestations. If we are successful tonight, we will be in touch with the spirit of Adolf Hitler."

An excited murmur ran through the audience.

"That will come later. For now, I must also inform you, in a preliminary way, that I am not the rabble-rousing demagogue bent on personal power that the liberals, radicals, and Commies would make me. Theirs is an old strategy: smear a man personally in order

124

to discredit his views. I stand for a consistent set of beliefs which are unassailable. Let them defame and misrepresent me. The attacks of treacherous swine are a measure of their malicious ignorance, stupidity, and fear.

"I used the word *ignorance*. People are unwilling to face unpleasant facts, so they attempt to bury or ignore them. But I shall present facts this evening that cannot be hidden or ignored, however inconvenient they may be to certain people.

He pulled down a large wall chart.

"Here is a chart of the world's population growth in the past ten years. The figures are a matter of public record, available from Washington."

The chart showed that Australia had the lowest population growth, less than one and a half million. Western Europe had slightly over three million; Communist Europe, almost four million; the United States, eight and two-thirds million; U.S.S.R. over eleven million; Latin America, forty-four million; Africa, sixty-four million; and Asia two hundred and fifty million.

"From these figures," Kleist went on, "it is clear that the white race is bent on suicide. At the same time that whites are deliberately limiting population growth through birth control and abortion, blacks and Asians are rapidly rising in numbers.

"This decline in the white race spells a decline in human civilization. As Hitler demonstrated, every aspect of culture, every product of art, science, and engineering is almost exclusively the product of civilization of Aryan creative power. The Aryans are the true founders of civilization on this earth. The blacks and Asians have accomplished almost nothing on their own."

Eric heard muted sounds of approval and satisfaction rippling through the audience; his own emotions were anger and outrage. Kleist was manipulating statistics and falsifying history to his own ends. Like all racists, his arguments had a surface plausibility aimed at demonstrating the superiority of the Caucasian race. It was an argument that had been punctured by the overwhelming consensus of social anthropologists; but it survived in the warped mentalities of those, like Kleist, to whom it was an article of faith.

Kleist's voice had grown in power and fervor. Once again he pointed to the chart. "More than 90% of the population growth in the last decade took place among the black, brown, and yellow races—who already comprise 80% of the world's population. At the present rate of decline, whites will constitute only 10% of the world's population in the year 2000. The planet will be overrun by teeming hordes of pestilential, grasping, inferior races. All on a planet whose natural resources are already being overtaxed and exhausted."

Kleist paused to wipe his brow. "I beg your attention to these statistics—insignificant as they may seem. For once we grasp their significance, they foretell a frightening chapter in human history.

"Hitler wrote in *Mein Kampf*, 'Nations that allow their people to be turned into mongrels sin against the Will of Nature.' Whenever Aryans have mingled their blood with an inferior race, it has resulted in the downfall of culture. Contamination of the blood has resulted in the death of all the great civilizations of the past. It is against the evolutionary plan for a superior race to mix with an inferior one. The inferior always outnumber

the superior. The superior can survive only through dominating the masses, bending them to their will. We must keep our racial stock pure, and increase our numbers!

"This is the lesson of these statistics. Arm yourselves with knowledge and facts. Be prepared to act. Act to preserve our Aryan heritage. Act on behalf of yourselves, your families, your nation—on behalf of the white race."

The audience rose to their feet and cheered wildly, ecstatically. Kleist had played upon their egos, making them feel important; they were special people. Standing next to Eric, Purdon was pumping his fists in the air, in a gesture of power and allegiance. Eric had a sick feeling in the pit of his stomach. He had never before encountered hatred on such a broad scale, hatred of human differences.

He had always felt enriched by his contacts with people of diverse ethnic backgrounds. Kleist's drivel about preserving the purity of Aryan blood made genetic nonsense. Human blood cannot be distinguished by race. Eric wondered whether Kleist would refuse a transfusion from a black, an Asian, or a Jew if he were bleeding to death. Eric realized that Kleist used the word "blood" as a metaphor; but his choice of words betrayed both his ignorance of biology and his readiness to exploit loaded terms.

When the audience's outburst had subsided, Kleist stepped down from the stage and began to mingle with the crowd.

Purdon nudged Eric. "He's something else, isn't he? I told you the Fuhrer is a gifted man."

128

Eric nodded sourly, caught himself, and forced a weak smile.

"Come on, get into the spirit of things."

"I guess I'm struck speechless," Eric said.

He was relieved to discover that not everyone shared the crowd's enthusiasm. A graying man to his right sat immobile, hands jammed in his pockets, face sullen and troubled. He looked out of place and resentful. Purdon gave him a brief, hard stare, then returned his attention to Kleist, who mounted the podium again.

"I shall now attempt to communicate with our spiritual leader, Adolf Hitler."

There was an audible intake of breath in the audience. All eyes were riveted on Kleist.

"If I am successful, he will speak through me, using my vocal cords to deliver a message. Although I shall be in a state of trance, the speech center in my brain will automatically translate his words into English—I can feel his presence. His spirit hovers near."

His words began to slur, as a dreamy, faraway look appeared in his eyes. His eyelids drooped. Slowly, his head sank forward until it rested on his chest. His breathing sounded like the snore of deep slumber. He appeared to be in a deep trance. Then a remarkable transformation came over his sagging features. The muscles in his face quivered and tightened. His eyes opened, and Eric saw something in their depths that was vicious, cunning, predatory. They burned with an intensity of passion that recalled films of Hitler addressing his legions.

Kleist struck a belligerent pose. When he spoke, his voice was dry and harsh.

"I, Adolf Hitler, speak to you through my dedicated disciple, Werner Kleist."

His voice began to soar in ringing tones. "During my lifetime I fought for a New Order in Europe. We must continue that struggle to establish a New Order—here in America. It is the destiny of the Master Race to come to power."

The words rapped out with savage fury.

"Evolution provides an iron Law of Nature, that the strongest and best must triumph. The Aryan race has the natural right to endure as the sole masters of mankind. In America they prattle of democracy. Democracy! Do you know what democracy is? Democracy is government by the dunderheaded majority—an inefficient form of government corrupt at its core. The masses are like children, an unthinking herd that has to be directed and controlled for its own welfare. It cannot be trusted to elect the best men for public office. Human progress is not founded on the multitude. One leader, the Fuhrer, must have absolute authority. Absolute! You have such a leader! Werner Kleist. In him you must vest your fate and your future. His decision shall be final in all matters.

"I must soon depart the earthly plane. Before I go, I leave with you these final words. You have been entrusted with a mission, a holy crusade to revive the spirit of fascism in America. You must obtain control of the government at the local and national levels. You must rid the country of foreign elements and inferior strains."

His fist came down repeatedly upon the lectern. "You have it within your power to overturn the government. I began with a small band of followers that grew into an irresistible tidal wave. Sow seeds of disunity among our enemies. Turn hatred into a potent weapon of social change. Do not be afraid to hate. Hate is a pure, cleansing emotion. Hate and destroy, before you are destroyed.''

"Hate! Hate! Hate!"

The audience chorused the words in a rabid, hypnotic chant. Carried away in a surge of raging emotion, their voices resounded deafeningly through the hall.

Goering shouted, "Heil Hitler!" and the audience took up the cry, booming the words in unison.

"Heil Hitler! Heil Hitler! Heil Hitler!"

Their shoes beat time to the rhythm of the chant.

In the midst of the tumult, Eric became aware of the man next to him. He was on his feet like the others, but he was not cheering. His eyes were like daggers aimed at Kleist's heart. He raised his voice. "Death to Hitler!"

His right hand was hidden inside his coat. In the next instant, a gun flashed in his palm. He cocked the hammer.

Instinctively, Eric seized his wrist, jerking it high in the air. A shot cracked out with a burst of flame and smoke, the bullet ripping through the ceiling. Eric managed to get both hands on the gun and yanked it out of the gunman's hand.

"That's not the way!" Eric shouted.

"Nazi pig!"

"Hurry. There's an exit on your right," Eric spoke into his ear. "Run!"

Cries broke out from all parts of the auditorium, as necks craned in their direction. Everyone was momentarily stunned into immobility; now they began to move. Kleist's front-row goon squad was clambering up the center aisle, shoving people aside in their eagerness to get at the gunman. Hands reached out to grab him. The gunman broke free and propelled himself toward the side exit. He was surprisingly fleet of foot for a solidly built man, and launched himself against the heavy double doors. They sprang apart, admitting a good gust into the stagnant air of the hall. Eric heard the man's footsteps running up the alley. Shouts rang out, followed by scuffling.

A voice that Eric recognized as the deputy sheriff's stood out above the hubbub: "Let's nail this guy the right way, by the book. It's safer all around."

There were vociferous objections and heated vows to "tear him apart." But Scagg urged them to let him handle it, and in the end, "law and order" prevailed.

Eric heard a police car tear off down the street. As its siren diminished, the khakis returned to the hall.

By this time, Eric was the center of a small circle of admirers. Purdon had an arm around his shoulder, and a clutch of girls fluttered about him, bubbling congratulations.

Kleist was standing on the stage with a glazed expression, as if he had just emerged from a reverie. The bogus generals formed a protective cordon around him.

Goebbels stepped off the stage and proceeded up the aisle toward Eric. "Come out here, Eric Thorne," he called. "Everyone would like to see you."

Eric hesitated.

"Don't be shy. The Fuhrer wants to extend his personal congratulations to you for your act of valor."

People stared at him with radiant smiles as encouraging hands nudged him out into the aisle. Goebbels took his arm, and they marched to the stage amidst a clamor of cheers and clapping.

As they mounted the podium, Goebbels said, "My Fuhrer, I have the pleasure of presenting Eric Thorne, our most promising young recruit. He is the one who subdued the gunman while you were in a trance."

Kleist shook Eric's hand. "I am most happy to meet you, Eric. It appears I owe my life to you. You are very brave."

"I am honored to meet you, my Fuhrer," Eric replied. "But I am undeserving of your kind words. I did no more than anyone else in my position would have done."

"Well spoken," Kleist said. "But you are too modest. Courage and decisiveness under fire are uncommon qualities. I would like to get to know you better. Tell me, what do you do?"

"I'm a student right now."

"What school do you attend?"

"Central High School in Ivy."

"I see. You live in Ivy?"

"Yes."

Kleist's eyes narrowed reflectively. "I have been formulating plans for a parade through Ivy. You might be the perfect man to direct it."

Eric swallowed. "I'm flattered by your confidence in me."

Kleist turned and addressed the audience. "I would like you to meet the young man who fought off the Zionist terrorist."

Zionist terrorist? There was no evidence the assailant was a Zionist or a Jew, Eric thought.

"May I present Eric Thorne, the newest recruit to the New Order. I am certain he will prove a credit to our organization."

The audience gave Eric an enthusiastic round of applause. He flushed and waved his hands.

"Seated among you are those who are here for the first time. Perhaps some of you wandered in out of curiosity. I trust your curiosity will ripen into a lifelong passion. You have seen an excellent example of the caliber of our members. If you would like to join our cause, see Mr. Ludwig at the back of the auditorium.

"Membership is not easy. We expect complete loyalty, dedication, and self-sacrifice. If you qualify, we welcome you into our ranks. We are rising in strength and gaining in numbers—in Germany, in Argentina, and in the United States. To all of you I wish good health, good fortune, and a New Order. *Auf Wiedersehen.*" He raised both hands in the air and received a tumultuous tribute from his acolytes.

Turning to Eric, he said, "I would like to meet with you tomorrow evening. I will make arrangements for someone to pick you up."

"Thank you," Eric said. "I look forward to it."

"Heil Hitler," Kleist saluted, walking briskly off the stage.

Eric returned his salute.

134

# 15 • *Important Assignment*

"I'm in a quandary, Alison."

"What's the matter?"

"I don't think I'm cut out to be a double agent," Eric said. "Acting the part of a Nazi is getting to me. Last night, at the lecture, when I stopped that man from shooting Kleist—"

"Yes?"

"I felt like a coward and a hypocrite. Now Kleist is planning a march through Ivy and wants me to set it up, after we discuss it tonight. What will people think?"

"It's not going to be easy."

"Eric Thorne a Nazi? It doesn't gel. They won't believe it—at first. It will be my job to convince them I'm a Nazi. Then they'll think I'm crazy. Soon they'll come to despise me."

"Just pretend you're an actor playing a part. It won't be the real Eric Thorne they despise, but the role you've created."

"It's like splitting yourself down the middle. I know I'm not that role, but they'll identify me with it. And I'll be unable to say, 'Look, I'm still the same old Eric Thorne.'"

"I'll know it, and Paul will know it. It's not the real you they'll hate, but a straw man—an identity you're assuming for a brief period. It's like the masks those Nazis wore. Once you take it off, you can resume your own life again."

"For me, though, it will never be the same again. People will never see me the way they used to—even if they believe I've come back to my senses."

"They'll probably think it was a phase you went through. You simply outgrew it—or maybe you had psychotherapy!"

"I hope so. Anyway, this is no time for me to waver."

"Not when you've just won the Nazis over."

"We'll see how long that lasts!"

Later that day, Eric received a call from Ludwig, the Party's Membership Chairman. Eric was to meet him in Millbrook at nine, on the corner of State and Euclid. From there, he would drive Eric to the hotel where Kleist was staying.

"Bring your sister along too," Ludwig suggested. "The Fuhrer would like to meet her."

Alison, who was listening in on the conversation, nodded her head.

"It's not every day you get to meet Adolf Hitler," she said after Eric had hung up.

"If he's in the mood to materialize," Eric answered. "After last night, he may have second thoughts. Even ghosts don't like being shot at."

136

Ludwig was waiting for them in a black sedan. Eric introduced him to Alison.

"Your sister has a very intelligent face," Ludwig observed.

"That's one of the nicest compliments I've ever received," Alison said. "Eric doesn't always appreciate my brain."

"You should hit it off real well with the Fuhrer. He's a real pushover for women of wit." Ludwig spoke with a slight German accent overlaid with an Oxford intonation. He looked to be about thirty-five, with blue eyes and light brown hair thinning at the temples.

"The Fuhrer usually stops at the Waverly Hotel when he's in town. It's just a short ride from here."

The Waverly, built in the thirties, retained a faded elegance absent in the functional architecture that characterized most of Millbrook. Kleist had a suite on the third floor.

As Ludwig predicted, Kleist's interest in Alison was immediate and expansive. Alison's eyes glinted in secret amusement at the older man's attentions.

He introduced Eric and Alison to his other guests. Sheriff Dolan; Ernst Kruger, a scientist; Herman Fuchs, an exponent of the martial arts; Klaus Schmidt, an Austrian financier; and Hans Eckart, "a distinguished World War II officer."

After toasting Alison's "charm and unstudied beauty," he suggested that they get down to work, and unfolded a street map.

"I have marked in red the central parade routes through Ivy."

Eric noticed that Kleist had traced the principal avenues circling the campus. His interest was concentrated on converting college students, as opposed to townspeople in peripheral areas.

"We will need a parade permit. Sheriff Dolan assures me this will not pose a problem. The matter of hooliganism is of more serious concern."

"I've already spoken with some police officials in Ivy," Dolan volunteered, "and they pledge a sizeable security force to protect our people."

Alison recalled her conversation with Eric after the abduction of the man in tan. They had speculated on possible Nazi infiltration of Ivy's police department.

"We don't want it too peaceful," Kleist explained. "We'd like to provoke some incidents, with police support to ensure our safety. If successful, the parade will focus nationwide attention on the Party."

Kleist appointed Eric to put the plan in motion. Tom Watson, a Midwest University student Party member, would assist him. The date of the parade was set for the following Monday.

Kleist then abruptly changed the subject to a scientific project in which he was keenly interested. "I will ask Dr. Kruger to describe it to you. What he's about to tell you is top secret. It must not go beyond the confines of this room. Is that understood?" The question was directed at Eric and Alison.

"Of course," Eric said.

Alison nodded her head in agreement.

"Are you familiar with the field of genetic engineering, in particular, cloning?" Kruger asked.

"We've heard about it," Eric answered.

"A clone is an exact copy or reproduction of an

138

organism. I understand that you and Alison are twins. Unlike a twin, whose genetic makeup is inherited from two parents, a clone is a duplicate offspring of only one individual. To create a clone, the procedure is as follows: A microsurgeon takes the nucleus of a body cell—for example, a skin cell—containing a full set of chromosomes, and inserts it into an egg cell whose nucleus has been removed. The resulting embryo is implanted in the uterus of a woman, where it is nurtured like the fertilized ovum produced by normal conception. After nine months, the mother conceives a duplicate offspring of the cloned individual. Theoretically, you can produce multiple copies of a single person that are identical in every respect. One futurist envisions an army of clones—hundreds of thousands of identical individuals all derived from the same donor."

"The scientific possibilities are breathtaking!" Kleist raved. "We could build a Master Race of cloned Nazi war heroes."

*Nazi war criminals,* Eric corrected him mentally.

"In my lecture yesterday, I spoke of the population explosion among black and yellow races, and the continuing decrease in white births. Cloning could redress the balance. Picture an army of clones of Field Marshal Rommel, the 'Desert Fox.' It would be an unbeatable juggernaut overrunning Asia and Africa, and then the entire world."

"But Rommel is dead," Eric objected.

"In theory, you could even create clones of the dead," Kruger informed them. "Scientists have known for years that as plant and animal cells die, tiny cell elements remain alive. While the death of a body's cells ends one human life, it doesn't end all life in the corpse. As long as the chromosomes are viable, new life can be produced."

"I used Rommel as an example only," Kleist explained. "We have no lack of live heroes from whom to choose. But it requires more research. So far, there is still no confirmed case of a human clone."

"This is where you come in, Eric," Kleist continued. "We will not merely be flaunting our colors next Monday, or demonstrating our numbers. The more publicity we attract, the more contributions we may expect. Mr. Schmidt has already contributed generously. Largely through his efforts, we have established a scientific foundation under Dr. Kruger's direction. Research is going forward, but we need additional sources of revenue. The rally will help achieve this."

Eric was impressed by the importance of the responsibility entrusted to him. "I'll do my best to carry it off successfully, Sir."

"I know you will," Kleist said.

"It won't be easy," Sheriff Dolan warned. "We can expect a lot of opposition."

Kleist brushed the remark aside. "Nothing worthwhile is achieved without effort and sacrifice." Kleist glanced at his watch. "I'm afraid I'm keeping you too late." He turned to Alison and clasped her hand in both of his.

"It was a pleasure to meet you," Alison said.

# 16 • *Guardian Angel*

---

**NAZI PARTY**

**FREEDOM MARCH**
for
**WHITE POWER**

Monday, April 14

Rally at Franklin Mall, 1 P.M.

---

The ad appeared in the *Ivy Press* and in the *Midwest Student News*. It was Thursday, and the march was scheduled for the following Monday.

As Eric folded up the newspaper, the doorbell rang.

"I'll get the door, Aunt Rose," Eric called. It was Tom Watson, the student Nazi to whom Kleist had referred. Eric opened the door.

There was nothing about Watson's appearance that betrayed his party affiliation. He looked like a typical Midwest University student. Dressed in jeans and a college sweater, he was of average height, with brown hair and even features. He had stacks of posters that Eric helped carry into the house.

"Hot off the press," Watson said. He pulled a poster off the top. It was a blowup of the ad, with the addition of a swastika.

"Nice job," Eric said.

"The swastika was my touch. It should really get to them. A symbol is often more provocative than language."

"I see your point," Eric said. He had the impression that Watson was ruffled that Kleist had passed him up in favor of the younger Eric.

"We should have enough to cover most of the town," Watson said.

"Suppose I take the south side—south of Jefferson. You take the north," Eric suggested.

"All right."

Watson started to leave. "Before you go," Eric said, "I'm curious to know how long you've been a Party member."

"Why?"

"No particular reason."

"About a year."

"After the march is over, we should get to know each other better," Eric said.

"I'd be glad to."

"Are you the only student member in Ivy?"

"Yes, but there are plenty who are ripe for the

picking. Most students' political views are amorphous and undeveloped. It just takes a push in the right direction."

"Are there Party members in the high school or university faculty?"

A suspicious look came into Watson's eyes. "Why are you pumping me? That question is not for me to answer. Ludwig is the only one who can tell you."

"I just thought it might be useful if someone on the faculty participated."

"I disagree. A professor can be most effective politically from a covert position. With his identity hidden, he can continue to influence students without fear of administrative opposition."

"I'll speak to Ludwig about it."

"You won't get anything from him," Watson said.

*So that's the way it works,* Eric thought. *These people are suspicious of everyone, even themselves.*

"I'll be leaving now," Watson said. He lifted a stack of posters and carried it out to his car.

"See you later," Eric called. Watson waved stiffly.

Eric took the other stack and shoved it into the trunk of his car. He headed for Jefferson Avenue.

As he began putting up the posters, Eric was surprised that his activity didn't attract more attention. He reasoned that student notices were a common sight around the campus, and people simply weren't curious. A few passers-by glanced casually in his direction, doing a double-take as the text sank in. They quickly looked away and quickened their pace.

One student whom Eric knew slightly walked up and read the sign. "You're kidding," he said.

"No, it's for real."

"Come on, it's a put-on. What fraternity are you working for?"

"Honestly, the sign means what it says."

"You mean you're a—?" The sentence hung in the air, incomplete.

"A Nazi." Eric nodded his head. "Try to make the parade on Monday."

The student backed away awkwardly. His jaws began to work, but nothing came out. With an embarrassed look, he turned and walked off.

Eric worked his way south, until he found himself in a rundown section of town. A few posters remained, and he proceeded to put them up.

He was suddenly aware of the hostile stare of two blacks standing across the street. They were about Eric's age.

"Hey, what you doing there, man?" one of them shouted.

It was self-explanatory, so Eric didn't bother answering.

They started toward him.

"I asked you a question!"

"It's my job," Eric said.

The other black edged a step closer to him. "What my friend means is you're in the wrong part of town. 'White power' doesn't sit well here. Get it?"

"I don't make the posters," Eric answered. "I'm just putting them up. It's my job."

"He smells like a Nazi!" the first black snapped.

"I don't want any trouble," Eric said.

"Well, you're just looking for it, honkey!"

By this time a group of blacks and Hispanics had gathered. The mood of the crowd was ugly.

The incongruity of the situation struck Eric, as if he were an observer watching himself at a distance. A young white, flaunting a Nazi swastika, appears in an underprivileged neighborhood proclaiming "white power." It was hate at first sight. How else could they react? How stupid of him not to have considered it! His problem, he realized, was that he didn't think like a Nazi. So he hadn't anticipated it. He was just going through the motions without living the part—and now the part had boomeranged.

A Hispanic man eyed him as if he had just crawled out of a crack in the sidewalk. "This hombre wants us to march in a Nazi parade!" His voice was incredulous.

Eric decided his best defense was stupidity. "It wasn't my idea! I just got stuck with the job of putting these up."

"And they told you to put up Nazi posters in this neighborhood? Caramba!"

"They just said, 'Put up the posters.' I was trying to get rid of 'em."

"Then throw them in the sewer where they belong." He pulled the posters down and tore them in half.

In the next instant, the crowd was grappling with the signs, clawing and rending them like sheets of living tissue. Children scooped up the confetti-like fragments and tossed them by handfuls into the air.

Then, in a kind of frenzy, the crowd whirled on Eric, heckling him from all sides.

"You're not as innocent as you seem."

"You're a hired Nazi flunky."

They pressed around him, eyes flaring angrily, hands reaching out.

"Let him alone!" someone shouted above the din.

The crowd milled uncertainly, parting as a black youth cleared a path toward the front.

It was Paul!

"What's going on here?" he demanded. "This is a friend of mine."

"He's a fascist pig!" a young black shot back.

"You're crazy. You don't know what you're talking about."

A Hispanic woman entered the fray. "He posts signs that say, 'Nazi Party Freedom March for White Power.' What do you think of that, huh?"

"I tried to explain it was a job I had to do," Eric said.

Understanding flashed across Paul's face. "I can't explain it now," he told the crowd. "But believe me, he's a good man."

"Nazi lover!"

"Uncle Tom!"

"Someday I'll be able to explain it. If you hurt him, you'll be making a big mistake."

The crowd seemed undecided, and somehow cheated.

"Let them go," a black man shouted from the rear. He was wearing a dark silk suit and a gray fedora. He looked well-heeled, and the crowd deferred to him. "Can't you see he's telling the truth?"

The crowd shrugged and reluctantly dispersed.

"Thank you, Mr. Mathews," Paul said. "It looked hairy for a while."

"Glad to be of help."

"Mr. Mathews, this is my friend, Eric Thorne."

"How do you do, Eric?"

They shook hands.

"Mr. Mathews is an attorney and the neighborhood troubleshooter," Paul said.

"I hope you know what you're doing, Eric," Mathews said, with a canny look. "I don't believe you're a Nazi, but you're onto something dangerous that can easily backfire. You just had an example of mass aggression. A crowd is an organism without a guiding conscience."

Eric had the feeling that Mathews saw right through him. Was he that transparent?

"Thank you," Eric said. "I'll keep it in mind."

Mathews looked at his watch, wished them luck, and walked off, kicking at a pile of confetti in his path.

"What are you up to?" Paul asked.

Eric brought him up to date on his recent activities.

"So now you're Kleist's protege, just as he was Hitler's."

"Yes, and it's tearing me up inside."

"I can imagine. But it won't be long before you know their entire operation, and you'll be able to nail them."

"I'll be glad when this march is over."

"I'll be there," Paul said. "If you need me, I won't be far away."

"No, stay out of it, Paul. We can't be seen together."

"I'll stay out of sight. But I'll still be around."

"Good enough. Now I know how it feels to have a guardian angel. Thanks for your help just now. It was getting rough."

"I'd stay away from this area for a while."

"I got the message," Eric said.

Paul wished him luck on Monday, and Eric hopped into his car.

When he arrived home, Alison greeted him with the news that the phone has been ringing off the hook. "People saw you putting up the posters, and they're angry. My ears were burning at the language some of them used. A reporter for the *Student News* wants to interview you. And the Administration office at the University phoned. You'd better get over there right away. Dr. Vaughn wants to see you."

"That's just great!" Eric said. Without another word, he turned around and walked out the door.

In the Dean's office, the receptionist stiffened at the mention of his name.

"I understand that Dr. Vaughn wants to see me."

"If you'll have a seat, I'll see if the Dean is available." She walked into his office.

She returned a minute later. "He will see you now." He was probably one of his father's best friends. How would he explain to Dr. Vaughn without revealing more than he dared at this time?

Dr. Vaughn looked up as Eric entered the office.

"Sit down, Eric. I'd like to ask you a few questions. First, how can you, a Christian young man, accept the hateful, ruthless ways of the Nazis?"

Eric looked down at the floor to avoid looking into Dr. Vaughn's puzzled and hurt eyes. The Dean continued speaking.

"Do you realize the vast difference between the message of hatred and superiority that the Nazis preach and the message of the gospel? How can you possibly believe both of them?"

"I understand that it is very difficult to be a Christian and a Nazi," Eric responded, still averting Dr. Vaughn's gaze.

"But you have nevertheless chosen to become a member of the Nazi Party, accepting their prideful ways and destructive philosophy. Is this true, Eric?"

Eric swallowed hard. "Yes, sir."

"I find it hard to believe that Randall Thorne's son has made this decision. Does your father know about this?"

"No, I haven't written to him about it."

"You're really serious about this. Not putting me on?"

"Yes, I'm serious."

"Randall will be terribly disappointed to know this. It's opposed to everything your father stands for. Why do you think he spends so much time helping in underdeveloped countries? It's not just a matter of his agricultural expertise, you know. He gives much of his time and energy—and money too—to help Christian missions provide instruction and agricultural technology to peoples all over the world—so they can grow food to feed the hungry of all tribes and nations. And he does it all in Jesus' name."

Dr. Vaughn stopped speaking and sat quietly. He seemed to be waiting for Eric to reply. Neither said anything for several seconds.

"I'm afraid I don't always see things my father's way," Eric finally responded.

"Apparently not. Is there a Nazi Party chapter

here on campus, as far as you know, Eric?'' Dr. Vaughn asked. "Please tell me the truth.''

"I don't believe there is a chapter here.''

"Then it's off campus. In Ivy?''

"No, sir.''

"Where is their headquarters?''

"I'm not at liberty to say, sir.''

Vaughn's hand came down hard on the newspaper. "Why didn't you consult me or someone else in administration here at the University before running this ad?''

"We have a valid city permit for the parade, Dr. Vaughn. I believe this is a municipal, not a University matter.''

"Any march held on any portion of this campus is a University matter. And, as the son of one of our distinguished professors, your conduct on and off the campus reflects on the University. You are accountable for that conduct.''

"Freedom of assembly is a constitutional guarantee,'' Eric answered. "If you abridge one party's freedom of expression, the Republican or the Democratic Party may be next. Where does the censorship stop?''

"I don't deny that the Nazis may be considered a legitimate party according to the American democratic system. But it sounds strange to hear you speak of freedom of expression. If the Nazis had their way, there would be no freedom of expression or of anything else in this country.''

"If you yell 'Fire!' in a crowded theater,'' Dr. Vaughn continued, "are you exercising a constitutional right or inciting a riot? Freedom is not always free. It car-

151

ries with it certain responsibilities. Your rally is incendiary in nature. It will disrupt the campus, and the city, and produce counter demonstrations, possibly violence. I can't order you to call it off, but I'm asking you to."

"I don't have the authority," Eric said.

"Then tell me who does. Who are your leaders?"

"I can't say. Not at this point."

Vaughn leaned forward. "Eric, if you're in some sort of trouble—if these people have a hold on you—you can take me into your confidence. I'll help you in every way I can."

"I'm sorry. I can't say any more now."

Vaughn's face hardened. "Then I'll have to—" He stopped without indicating what action he had in mind.

"May I go now?"

"Yes. Please do."

Eric left, feeling an inch taller than a snake in the grass.

When he got home, he sank into a chair exhausted.

"That reporter from the college paper phoned again," Alison informed him.

"If he calls again, tell him I'm not interested."

"But you're passing up an opportunity to publicize the march."

"Hang the march! I'm not going to be a spokesman for those bloody Nazis. I'll ask Tom Watson. He'd just love to sound off, I'm sure."

"Don't forget the phone is still tapped. If they hear me turn down the reporter, it won't sit well with them."

"Then don't answer it. Better still—" He jumped up, unscrewed the base of the phone, and pulled out the tap. "There!" He flung it on the floor and stamped on it.

Alison shrank back, a little frightened. "Eric, are you all right?"

"Sure I'm all right. Dad is on the verge of being dismissed from the University, people hate my guts; they think I've turned my back on the Lord to join up with the devil; and—"

There was a sudden shattering sound as a rock flew through the window in a shower of splintering glass.

A cry rang out. "Racist pig!"

Eric ran to the window. A car stood double-parked, its motor running. He couldn't identify the driver. As he went to open the door, he heard the squeal of tires, and the car took off down the street.

# 17 • The Unmasking

The police, wielding billy clubs, were pushing back the demonstrators as they strained against the ropes.

With the aid of some khaki-clad reinforcements, Eric and Watson put the final touches on a dais raised above Franklin Mall.

Insults rained upon them from hecklers in the crowd. Eric was anxious to get the job done and return home. Kleist would be there by now. The thought of the Fuhrer alone with Alison made him sick. One of Kleist's assistants had phoned earlier that morning, suggesting that Kleist stop over at Eric's house before the rally. Eric was in no position to refuse.

How would he ever explain this man to Aunt Rose? Or any of the other men, for that matter? It was difficult enough trying to catch all the phone calls, to explain why someone might throw a rock through the window, and to keep her calm midst all the other strange happenings.

What worried him most was that neither he nor Alison would be able to keep her from calling Gramps in Washington much longer and telling him about the goings-on. That would ruin everything, because then the FBI, the Secret Service, and the police force would be swarming all over the place.

Eric climbed down from the dais and proceeded up the path cleared by the police. Watson and the other Nazis followed close behind him, shooting malevolent glances at the angry protesters.

A young man leaning over the rope struck out at Watson, who staggered back, holding his mouth. Fists began to fly, but the police intervened, and the Nazis left amidst a flurry of raucous jeers and threats.

The mob would be waiting when they returned with Kleist, Eric thought. The rally was just an hour away.

The Nazis piled into Eric's car, and they drove off.

Watson dabbed at his cut lip with a handkerchief. "Marxist fanatics!" he stormed.

One of the khakis snarled, "I hope we catch 'em some time on our own turf."

"We'll bust 'em up good," another growled.

Eric continued driving in silence.

They were greeted by a line of pickets outside Eric's house. The pickets waved placards reading "DEATH TO THE NAZIS!" and "THE NAZIS ARE ROACHES. EXTERMINATE 'EM!" Not stopping to read all of the signs, Eric parked down the block.

The khakis reached inside their pockets.

"No weapons!" Eric ordered.

They protested hotly.

"That was a condition of the march," Eric insisted.

"We don't want bloodshed. Remember, those are students out there."

"You fight them off yourself then," Watson shot back. "Bare-handed."

"Anyone harming a student will answer to the Fuhrer himself. I'll report the first man I see with a weapon."

"Since when do you give orders?" Watson demanded. "You're just a Johnny-come-lately."

"The Fuhrer put me in charge of this operation. You will follow my instructions or face Party discipline."

"Some people are too softhearted to be Nazis," Watson muttered.

Eric was relieved to see a patrol car pull up in front of his house. Three policemen stepped out. The senior officer addressed the marchers. "Do you have a permit to picket here?"

A bearded young man stepped forward. "Who says we need one?"

"The law does."

"We're just walking. Sidewalks are for walking."

"You're creating a disturbance. This is private property. You are ordered to disperse immediately."

The picketers promptly sat down on the pavement.

"Please don't make me call the paddy wagon," the officer said. "It will spoil your day and mine, and you'll miss the rally to boot."

The bearded youth considered this argument. "All right, gang, let's shake it," he called out.

The others stood up and tramped off in the direction of the campus.

Eric waited till the police left before getting out

of the car. The Nazis followed him into the house. Some of Kleist's bodyguards were standing inside the entrance.

Kleist was fuming. "Communist swine! In Germany we knew how to deal with their kind."

Watson seized the opportunity. "We wanted to rough them up, but the Thorne in our side stopped us."

Kleist glanced from Watson to Eric, weighing the antagonism between the two. "Altered circumstances demand new strategies. It would not be wise under present conditions."

Alison changed the subject. "Anyone for coffee?"

The khaki squad flocked around the buffet table, with Alison the center of attention.

"I have already imposed too much on your sister's hospitality," Kleist said. "On such short notice. She is a charming hostess."

"Everything is set up in the mall," Eric told him. "The mikes are in place. As expected, demonstrators are out in force, but the situation is under control. A television crew is standing by."

"Good. This is my first outdoor appearance—a testing ground. From here, we move on to other sites near campuses across the heartland of America."

A car horn sounded outside. Kleist went to the window. A fleet of limousines filled with Nazi members took up the entire street.

Kleist cleared his throat. "Shall we proceed?"

The Nazis poured outside and into the cars.

Kleist halted on his way to the lead car. "Where is Alison? Isn't she coming?"

Eric thought fast, but was unable to invent an appropriate excuse for her to remain behind.

Standing behind the door, she gave a groan, then composed her features and went outside. "I was just putting on some make-up. Sorry to keep you waiting."

"Make-up cannot improve upon natural beauty," Kleist observed. "Come with us in the first car."

Eric got in the back, and the cortege took off. By the time they arrived, Franklin Mall was overflowing with people. A loud outcry went up as the Nazis, wearing swastika armbands, streamed out of the limousines. Picketers attempted to break through the police line, and a few scuffles started. The police subdued the rowdier demonstrators to cries of "Police brutality!" One of the protesters hurled a rock through the windshield of a parked limousine. A few Nazis started for him, but police came between them to maintain an uneasy semblance of order.

Kleist strode through the center of the mall with ceremonial dignity, his bodyguards forming a flying wedge around him. Eric stood up on the dais and tested the microphones. "Testing, one, two, three." His appearance was greeted with loud boos. But the most deafening chorus was reserved for Kleist himself as he prepared to speak. Placards rose in the air, and the crowd's hissing lashed out like a whip.

Kleist stood erect, gazing out contemptuously at the excited throng. He held up his hand for silence. The crowd continued to jeer.

"Are you afraid to listen?" his amplified voice boomed out.

The crowd responded with angry denunciations.

"I bring you racial pride."

"Go back to Germany!" someone shouted.

"And surrender America to the blacks, the Asians, the Jews? Aren't you tired of hearing blacks rant about 'black power'? I offer you white power, white pride." The pitch of his voice was rising. His words were clipped, exploding from his lips.

"You're a racist throwback," someone yelled.

"Hate monger!" A black student shook his fist.

"Did you know that Britain has more than a million black voters, but not one black man in the House of Commons? And there has never been a black President of the United States. Or a Jewish President. Why, I ask you? Because you wouldn't trust the highest office in the land to a black or a Hebrew. That's why!"

A Midwest professor raised his voice. "This— gentleman makes an arrogant and automatic assumption of superiority based on race. It is erroneous—"

Before he could complete his remark, a group of khaki hecklers shouted him down. Kleist attempted to gain control of the spotlight again. But his voice was drowned in a sea of catcalls.

Then something occurred that Eric had not bargained for. He could hardly believe his eyes. Into the heart of this angry scene strode a procession of masked men—the Nazi generals! The crowd quieted in astonishment.

*What stupidity!* Eric thought to himself. The mob was already half crazed with anger. Why trot out the most detested objects of that hatred, the very symbols of fascist militancy?

*Perhaps Kleist intended to provoke a riot from the very beginning. Did he hope to demonstrate that his opponents were more intolerant than he?* Eric wondered.

159

*Or was publicity the overriding consideration?* Eric recalled Kleist's remark that he wanted to focus nationwide attention on the Party. But this was sheer lunacy!

The man disguised as Goering cried, "Order! Order!" in a loud, commanding voice.

He and the other mock generals marched up to the podium beside Kleist. By now the crowd had recovered their voices, and were shouting imprecations, and shaking their fists.

An egg hurled from the crowd met its target squarely on Himmler's face. He rocked backward, with yolk dripping down onto his freshly starched uniform.

A hail of eggs splattered the podium before police could subdue the marksmen. The generals retreated in disarray, leaving Kleist a solitary figure standing ramrod-stiff above the multitude.

Himmler was halfway down the steps from the dais when a surge of students pushed through the ropes into his line of retreat. As police grappled with protesters, one of them darted up to Himmler, pinned him against the stairs, and ripped off his mask.

"Professor Richter!" A girl pointed at the unmasked scholar, her eyes wide with shock and embarrassment. Richter, an Egyptologist, was on the staff of Midwest's history department.

Richter flinched before the student's gaze, then drew himself up with dignity and proceeded down the stairs.

Meanwhile, a flock of demonstrators had ambushed the other generals and were busy unpeeling their masks. Standing in the crowd, a gray-haired man with sober, weather-beaten features watched the operation with particular interest. As Heydrich's mask was removed, the observer suddenly charged forward, crashing past the bystanders, and stared straight into the unmasked face. Heydrich shrank before the intensity of his accusing eyes.

"General Streicher! We meet at last!"

Heydrich's face crumpled. "How dare you?" he shrieked. "Are you insane? My name is not Streicher."

"I've waited many years for this, Streicher," the man persisted. He rolled up his shirt sleeve. A series of numbers was stamped on his forearm. "Do you recognize me, Streicher? My name is Martin Engel. I was a prisoner at your camp."

The color left the general's face. His eyes darted desperately from side to side. "You have the wrong man. My name is Gustav Ehrlich. I'm an actor, hired for the occasion to impersonate Heydrich."

Engel ignored his remark. He turned to some students. "Please hold this man. He's wanted for murder."

The man whom Engel called Streicher struggled to break free from the students hemming him in, as Engel signaled to a policeman.

The officer approached cautiously.

"Officer, my name is Martin Engel. Thirty years a Nazi hunter." He produced a passport confirming his identity. "This man is an escaped Nazi war criminal, a former concentration camp commandant. His name is Karl Streicher."

Streicher vehemently protested his innocence. "I don't know what he's talking about. He has me confused with someone else. Here, look at my visa." It bore the name of Gustav Ehrlich.

The policeman asked Engel if he was certain.

"I'll stake my life on it. I'm prepared to prefer charges against him. I've been tracking him for over five years. He was believed dead until one of our agents spotted him in Paraguay six years ago. He's been one step ahead of us at every turn—until today." He turned to Streicher. "You couldn't resist the temptation to play general again, could you, Streicher?"

The policeman took out a pair of handcuffs. "I'm taking you into custody." He read Streicher his constitutional rights. "If Mr. Engel is mistaken, we can clear it up at the station."

"I will sue for false arrest!" Streicher screamed. "I'll have your badge! I have influence!"

The policeman asked Engel if he recognized any of the other unmasked generals. Engel shook his head.

"Then I'll have to let them go. Okay, buddy, come on." The policeman hustled Streicher through the crowd, with Engel running interference at his side.

Kleist was still standing on the podium, his fists pounding the lectern, his lips framing words that no one heard. Someone had disconnected the microphone cables. He beckoned to his bodyguards. "Get me out of here."

They took him in tow, fleeing across the back of the mall, and retreating to the parked limousines, as police quelled the large surge of demonstrators.

Eric searched desperately for Alison. He found her waiting near the lead car.

"Get in," Kleist called to them. "Quickly!"

Eric bundled Alison inside and jumped in beside her.

"The swine will pay for this!" Kleist ranted as the car roared off down the street.

162

# 18 • *Child Hostage*

## 5 Injured, 6 Arrested
## at Nazi Party Rally

Special to Midwest Student News

IVY, Illinois, April 15—
A Nazi Party rally held in Franklin Mall erupted into a near-riot as police attempted to quell clashes between Nazi supporters and counter-demonstrators.

About four hundred people attended the rally. Five received minor injuries in fist fights and scuffles between opposing groups. Two non-student protesters and three Nazis were arrested for disorderly conduct.

One Nazi, identifying himself as Gustav Ehrlich, was arrested on suspicion of being the alleged Nazi war criminal, Karl Streicher. Upon verification of Streicher's identity by famed Nazi hunter Martin Engel, Streicher was remanded to the custody of the

163

Department of Justice. A spokesman indicated that the Department planned action to deport Streicher, an illegal alien, to West Germany, where he will stand trial for alleged war crimes committed at the Lublin concentration camp.

In a veiled threat, an unidentified Nazi Party member promised "retaliatory measures" if Streicher was not released immediately.

Werner Kleist, self-proclaimed Fuhrer of the Nazi Party, was interrupted repeatedly as he attempted to address the gathering. His speech was abruptly terminated when demonstrators began hurling eggs at Kleist and a coterie of supporters masquerading as former Nazi generals.

Kleist, a former member of the Nazi *Jugend,* emigrated to the United States after World War II, where he became known as a self-styled psychic.

Plans for a so-called "Freedom March for White Power" were canceled as Kleist and his cohorts hastily left the rally. Eric Thorne, a student at Central High and chief rally organizer, was unavailable for comment. Thorne is the son of Professor Randall Thorne, agronomist on the faculty of the School of Agriculture.

Reading the article renewed the rage Kleist had felt the previous day. After dropping Eric and Alison off at their home, he had gone directly to the warehouse outside of Millbrook. After a fitful night, the "Fuhrer" made one telephone call before summoning his remaining generals to an early meeting.

Putting the newspaper aside, he shouted, "We must rescue Streicher immediately. He is vital to our cause."

"But how?" Goering asked. "It would be suicide to try to free him from the federal authorities."

164

"Not by force, you idiot!" screamed Kleist. "There is a much easier and more effective way. Streicher will be released to us within forty-eight hours."

"Tell us your plan," said Himmler.

"It's quite simple," Kleist replied. "We will exchange our hostage for Streicher. The Justice Department will be given the option of freeing him or being responsible for the death of an innocent person."

"But we don't have a hostage," protested a puzzled Goebbels.

"Not yet, dumkopf! But we will. We soon will."

Dick Tracy and Clark Kent motioned through the front window of the gray Pontiac parked on Highland Drive.

"Hey, Cindy!" Tracy called.

Eight-year-old Cindy Vaughn, daughter of the University Dean of Students, turned toward the car.

"Your father asked us to pick you up. Your brother Charles had to stay late for some track workout." Tracy opened the front door.

Cindy walked over to the car. "Who are you?"

"I'm Dick Tracy, and this is my pal, Clark Kent. You know him—he's Superman."

"No, he's not. You're wearing masks, aren't you? Is it a game?"

"You're a smart girl," Kent answered. "Not everyone would have noticed."

"It's not even Halloween. Are you going to some kind of costume party?"

"Sure, that's it. You guessed it. Would you like to come along?"

165

"I can't. I have a dentist appointment."

"Hop in the car," Tracy said. "We'll take you there."

"Charles told you where the office is?"

"Yeah. But we'd better hurry, so we won't be late."

"Well, I guess it's all right if Charles said so." Cindy slid in beside him.

Tracy leaned over and pulled the door shut as Kent gunned the motor.

"Why did you pick Dick Tracy and Clark Kent?" Cindy asked.

"We're good guys," Tracy answered with a high-pitched laugh.

"The other drivers are the bad guys," Kent added.

Cindy stared out the window. "This isn't the way to the dentist's office. It's back there." She pointed through the rear window.

"This is a short cut," Kent said.

"It isn't! I know the way. Turn around!"

Kent ignored her.

Cindy stared hard at the immobile faces of the men beside her. "You're kidnappers, aren't you?"

"Kidnappers! Where did you learn a word like that?" Tracy asked.

"We're your uncles, Clark and Dick," Kent said. "We're going to take good care of you."

"You're not my uncles. You're kidnapping me, and kidnapping is a crime." She tilted her head bravely. "Take me home. At once!"

"Her little highness," Tracy snickered.

"Please take me home." Cindy began to cry.

"Shut your trap, kid," Tracy barked. "I hate blubbering females."

"I'm not a female! I'm a child," Cindy sobbed. She wriggled over and pressed her mouth to the window. "Help! Help!"

Tracy pulled her squirming back from the window. "Look, kid, no one can hear you. Be quiet or you'll get hurt!"

Cindy tossed her chin up defiantly. "I know why you're wearing masks," she said. "You're afraid I'll remember your faces."

"Pretty bright."

"If you let me go now, I promise I won't tell anyone."

"Pipe down or we'll tape your mouth shut," Kent threatened.

Cindy began to cry. "The police will catch you. You'll see."

They were on the outskirts of Ivy. Kent turned onto Route 36 headed for Millbrook.


Susan Vaughn glanced anxiously at the wall clock in Dr. Morse's tastefully furnished office. Cindy was already fifteen minutes late for her dental appointment. What was keeping her? Charles must have been held up in traffic. She got up and looked out the window.

Dr. Morse's nurse entered the waiting room. "Cindy still not here, Mrs. Vaughn?"

"No. I'm getting worried. May I use your phone?"

"Certainly."

Susan dialed her home number. The housekeeper answered.

"Hello, Ellen. This is Mrs. Vaughn. I'm waiting for Cindy at the dentist's office. Do you recall what time Charles left the house with Cindy?"

"He didn't come by here, Mrs. Vaughn. I haven't seen either of them."

"Didn't show up? What's wrong with that boy? Cindy must still be waiting for him. Ellen, I'll call Central High. Maybe he's been delayed. If you see him, tell him Cindy is waiting to be picked up at school." Her hand trembled as she put down the receiver.

"Would you please phone a cab for me?" she asked the nurse. "Charles probably forgot to stop for Cindy. I let him use my car on the condition that he pick her up from school and bring her here today."

"I'll phone a cab."

Ten minutes later, the taxi arrived. They drove to the corner where Charles was to pick up Cindy. Some people were sitting on a bench. Susan got out and asked them whether they had seen a little blonde girl. Not while they were there, they answered. Susan was beginning to worry. She dashed into a corner store. The owner hadn't noticed a girl of Cindy's description. She ran into the next store. The cashier remembered seeing a little girl. Had she seen anyone pick her up? Not that she recalled.

Susan asked the driver to circle the block. They combed the entire neighborhood. Frantic, she phoned the house again, then the dentist. Then she phoned her husband's office. He was at a conference, and his secretary was reluctant to interrupt him.

"It's an emergency!" Susan cried hoarsely, emotion choking her voice.

"All right, Mrs. Vaughn. I'm sorry, I didn't realize. Please hold the line."

Cindy was so fragile—like a Hummel figure. Susan always chided herself for being overprotective. Now she was gone. Someone had taken her. An unbalanced woman who desperately wanted a child. Or a child molester—

"Cindy's missing! And I can't locate Charles anywhere!"

"Have you found her?"

"Please let her be alive! Lord, please!" Vaughn prayed under his breath.

The two detectives entered the house with a professional calm that Vaughn found more disconcerting than reassuring.

"Not yet, Mr. Vaughn," Burke, the taller man, answered.

"Do you have any leads?"

Burke's expression was noncommital. "Nothing tangible yet."

"Did you find our son, Charles?"

"Yes, we located him in Newport Hospital, unconscious. A patrolman found him this afternoon slumped over the wheel of his car. He took a blow to the head."

"What happened to him? Is he all right? Why didn't someone call us?" The questions poured from Dr. Vaughn's lips.

"The report that we've received is that Charles is still unconscious. Seems to be a concussion."

"What happened to him? Did he have an accident? Where was he when—?"

"Dr. Vaughn, we don't know any of the details.

When he comes to, we can question him," an officer explained.

"Who's the doctor? What hospital did you say he's in? I must go to him." The words poured from Vaughn, one after another, without waiting for anyone to respond.

"I need to go to the hospital—to be with Charles," Dr. Vaughn said suddenly, as if realizing at that moment the whereabouts and condition of his seventeen-year-old son. "Excuse me, gentlemen."

"Dr. Vaughn, before you go, there are a few questions we need to ask you." The detective spoke with gentleness.

Vaughn slumped into a chair, his face crumpled like the portrait on a used dollar bill.

"Do you know anyone who might have a personal motive for taking Cindy?"

"Of course not."

"For this attack on your son?"

"No, I can't imagine anyone disliking Charles."

"Do you have any enemies?" Daniels asked.

"As a University administrator, I've had differences with people—but no, certainly no enemies."

"How about your wife?"

"You're barking up the wrong alley, Mr. Daniels. My wife doesn't have a previous husband, and there are no spurned lovers lurking in the background. I'm sorry; my nerves are on edge. I realize you have to ask these personal questions, but they're irrelevant to Cindy's apparent abduction and to Charles' being attacked."

"Other agents are working on the case, Mr. Vaughn," Daniels said. "About six hours have passed since

170

Cindy's disappearance, and there is still no ransom demand. The kidnappers may want to work up your anxiety for a bigger bit. But other motives besides money have to be considered."

"I'm not a wealthy man, but I'll pay anything they ask. I'll scrape it together somehow. I want your pledge that you won't interfere."

"You're getting ahead of the game, Mr. Vaughn. Let's discuss it after the contact—if there is one."

"I'm just trying to anticipate—"

The phone clanged. Vaughn leaped to his feet.

"If it's the kidnapper, keep him on the line as long as possible."

Vaughn picked up the phone. His tense expression changed to disappointment. "Yes, they're here. It's for you." He handed the receiver to Burke.

"Burke here." He listened intently, a flicker of anger appearing in his eyes. "Yes, I understand. I'll get back to you." He hung up.

"Mr. Vaughn, now try to be calm and listen."

"She's dead!" Vaughn guessed.

"No," Burke responded. "It's nothing like that." *The Tribune* just received a call from someone demanding the immediate release of the Nazi, General Streicher, with safe passage to Paraguay. He said your daughter will be kept as a hostage until this is done."

"They're madmen! Using a child as a political pawn!" He fought for self-control.

"The Nazi Party denies any responsibility for the kidnapping, according to one of their spokesmen, and the caller didn't identify himself as a member. We can assume the Party's complicity, but we can't prove it without concrete evidence. It could be the work of fanatics acting on their own initiative—people on the lunatic fringe.''

"That's a comforting thought!'' Vaughn sneered.

"He said that in future communications he'll use the name 'Dick Tracy.' ''

"It's all so unreal. What made them pick up my child? Wait a minute. I just had a thought. You asked me whether I had any enemies. You were considering the possibility of revenge. It didn't occur to me before, but I clashed with one of our professor's sons, a Nazi Party member and Central High student over the parade a few days before the rally. I advised him that his active participation could result in serious problems for his father. When he refused to cooperate, I threatened to call in the police.''

"What's his name?''

"Eric Thorne.''

"We'll have the police pick him up—if he's still around.''

# 19 • *Confession Time*

The word BULLETIN flashed on the television screen.
"We interrupt this program for a special report. Cindy Vaughn, eight-year-old daughter of Midwest University's Dean of Students, Dr. Russell Vaughn, was kidnapped early this afternoon while waiting for her brother to pick her up after school. Charles Vaughn, the brother, seventeen, is in guarded condition in Newport Hospital where he was taken after being found unconscious in his car near Central High School. He is reported to be suffering from a concussion.

A telephone call from an unidentified person claimed the child is being kept hostage pending the release and expatriation of the alleged Nazi war criminal, Karl Streicher, to Paraguay.

Justice Department proceedings to deport Streicher for trial in West Germany are presently underway. A Department spokesman had no immediate comment, but sources close to the attorney general's office indicated that it was government policy not to bow to blackmail. This is Peter Nichols reporting from Ivy, Illinois, for KBC News.''

Eric felt as if the roof had caved in on him. He had been watching television with Alison when the report came in.

"Those psychos! They won't stop at anything."

"I know the little girl," Alison said. "She just started taking piano lessons from my teacher, Mrs. Kjeldsen. The poor child must be frightened to death."

"I have a hunch where they've taken her," Eric said.

"The warehouse! The place where Fred Purdon took you blindfolded."

"Right. Their secret headquarters. They have a tremendous arsenal there, if they decide to fight it out with the police. Speaking of police, they're bound to come for me now. I'm so entangled with the Nazis that they might book me on suspicion of conspiring to kidnap the child."

"But it's not true!"

"What could I tell them, that I'm not really a Nazi? After the rally, who would believe me? Even if they don't have any evidence, they might cross-examine me all night. I can't tell them where that place is anyway. I have to find it. That's the only way I can help Cindy."

"If you run away now, it will look like a confession of guilt."

"But it's the only way to clear myself of suspicion, by finding the child and blowing the whistle on the Nazis. Time is precious. I can't afford to waste it fending police questions."

"Then we'll find the warehouse together."

"I'll need your help, Alison. You'll have to drive me blindfolded through the same area Purdon did. I'm banking that something will stand out—a distinctive background noise, the feel of a road's surface—something to guide me to the place. I think we should ask Paul to come along. We might need him."

As they were talking, they heard a car pull up. Alison ran to the window. "It's the police."

"C'mon, let's duck out the back way."

They bounded to the rear of the house.

Alison stopped at the door. "Do you think anyone's out there?"

"They haven't had time," Eric said, pulling the door open. The yard was hushed except for a solitary cricket.

They ran along the backs of the houses. As they came out on a sidestreet, the shrill note of a police whistle rang out, followed by the crunch of footsteps pounding on gravel. They doubled back to the corner, where Eric's car was parked. Clambering inside, Eric meshed the gears and pressed the accelerator to the floor. The whistle's strident peal pursued them down the street.

After putting a few blocks behind them, Eric swerved sharply. Moving in and out of sidestreets, at a careful twenty-five mile an hour speed—so as not to attract further police attention—they followed a twisting, chaotic route to Paul's house.

"Those crazy Nazis. They'd better not do anything to harm that little girl!" Eric growled under his breath.

As the car slid to a halt, Eric started to get out, but Alison's hand on his arm stopped him.

"We're running around like crazy people ourselves, Eric. Let's not do another thing till we talk to the Lord."

"Okay. You first."

"Our Father," Alison began, "You know we're up to our necks in this mess. We do so very much want to help get things straightened out. But we can't do it without Your help. It's so easy for us to make things worse rather than better. You know all about little Cindy—where she is, and those cruel men who have kidnapped her. Please keep her safe. Be a comfort to her parents, and bring her back safely. Thank You, Lord."

"I know I'm responsible for a lot of this trouble, Lord," Eric added. "Forgive me for the wrong things I've done. I do need Your help. Most of all, I want things to come out right. Help us, now, to find our way to that warehouse. Thank You, Lord. In Jesus' name. Amen."

With that, Eric bounded out of the car. Mrs. Tompkins answered his knock at the door.

"Hello, Mrs. Tompkins. Paul home?"

"I believe so—Paul!" she called upstairs.

"Yes?"

"Eric's here."

"Thank you," Eric said. He sprinted up the steps.

"Hey, buddy, what's up?" Paul was on the landing.

"Have you heard the news about the kidnapping?"

"What kidnapping?"

Eric quickly filled him in, and asked for his help in locating the warehouse.

Without a word, Paul zipped on his windbreaker. "Come on. What are we waiting for?"

As they trotted downstairs, Eric said, "They must have a make on my car by now. Can you borrow someone else's?"

"I'll ask Mrs. Tompkins. I sometimes use her car to run errands."

He knocked at her door. "Mrs. Tompkins, it's me, Paul."

Even before she opened the door, Paul asked, "May I borrow your car for a while? I'll put gas in it and have it washed. We'll get it back to you tonight."

"Sure," she replied, handing Paul the car keys. "Be careful now—and get me a loaf of whole wheat bread while you're out."

They ran outside. Paul waved a greeting to Alison.

"We're going in Mrs. Tompkins' car," Eric explained to her as Paul backed the car out of the garage.

"Wait," Eric said. "The police may spot my car here. It could easily connect us. I'd better park it away from the house."

Eric got in the car and drove it down the street, with Paul behind him. Then he locked the car and got in beside Paul and Alison.

"I'll drive," Paul said. "The police won't be looking for someone of my description."

"Lead on," Eric said.

"Just tell me when you want to be blindfolded."

"Not till we've passed Millbrook."

As they came onto the highway, it began to drizzle lightly. A thin film of mist settled on the windshield, clinging like translucent gauze. They lapsed into an uneasy silence, gazing straight ahead along the white glare of the headlights cleaving the darkness.

Paul switched on the radio, turning the dial to an all-news station. After a brief weather report, the announcer gave an update on the kidnapping.

"In response to the demand for the release of alleged Nazi war criminal, Karl Streicher, by the kidnappers of eight-year-old Cindy Vaughn, Martin Engel, famed Nazi hunter, has offered himself as a substitute. A spokesman for the Justice Department indicated that Streicher's impending deportation to West Germany is nonnegotiable. Appearing on national television, Engel made the following statement:

" 'My name is Martin Engel, Nazi hunter. Since 1950, I have tracked down thirty-eight Nazi war criminals and brought them before the bar of justice. To the kidnappers of Cindy Vaughn, I address the following remarks.

" 'You will never obtain the release of Karl Streicher by keeping the child hostage. The United States government is adamant in its refusal to negotiate political and legal issues with kidnappers. It will not bow to your demand under any conditions. I have it on the highest authority that this stand is irrevocable. However, in return for the child's release, I offer myself as a substitute for Streicher. If you are agreeable to it, contact *The Tribune* under the same name used in your previous communication. I urge you to do so at once. Details of the exchange will be worked out on mutually acceptable terms.

" 'Once I am in your custody, the child must be released unharmed immediately. If you fail to release her, or any harm comes to her, my agents throughout the world will hunt you down, each and every one of you, and exact the

178

ultimate penalty. I make this solemn vow, with God as my witness.'

"The parents of Cindy Vaughn have accepted Engel's offer, and have received assurances from the FBI that it will cooperate in the exchange.

"Following Engel's television appearance, the Police Department of Ivy, Illinois, issued a warrant for the arrest of Eric Thorne, a Nazi student organizer attending Central High School. Thorne is wanted for questioning in connection with the kidnapping."

"Don't worry," Paul said. "You'll be cleared."

"I don't think prison life would agree with me," Eric answered.

"That's a terrific gesture on Engel's part," Alison spoke up. "Not many people would be willing to sacrifice their lives in a similar situation."

"Do you think the Nazis will accept his offer?" Paul asked.

"It's the best offer they'll get," Eric said. "Snaring Engel would not only be a feather in their cap; it's a chance to avenge his capture of their comrades. I'm sure Kleist would love to get his hands on Engel."

They were a mile from Millbrook when another bulletin came on the air: "*Tribune* publisher Gordon Craig has just divulged that the kidnappers of Cindy Vaughn have agreed to release her in exchange for Martin Engel, Nazi hunter. Precise details of the exchange were not disclosed, but Craig indicated that the abductors promised to release the girl onto a public thoroughfare after their representatives pick up Engel. The abductors warned that any attempt to follow their confederates would result in grave consequences to the child. The exchange is expected to take place sometime tonight.''

"If we find Cindy before they make the exchange, we can save Engel's life," Eric said tensely.

"We have to be careful, though," Alison cautioned. "It could jeopardize the child."

"Who can believe those Nazis?" Paul said. "They might not carry through with their end of the deal."

The Millbrook exit came into view.

"Drive on past," Eric said.

After several miles, they came to a wooded area. "I remember this place," Eric said. "This is where Purdon tried to kill a squirrel that ran across the road. There's a dirt road straight ahead. We should hit it pretty soon."

"There it is," Paul said.

"Okay, make a right here."

They turned onto a bumpy road that ran past an old construction site.

"As I recall, the road cuts into an industrial area a few miles down."

After a short while, they came upon a gloomy row of factories and warehouses.

"Stop over there," Eric cried, "across the street. In front of that building."

"The one that says, 'Paragon'?"

"Yes."

Paul parked the car in the shadow of the warehouse.

"This is where Purdon blindfolded me," Eric said.

Paul took a large opaque handkerchief and wound it around Eric's eyes. "See anything?"

"Not a smidgen."

"Now what?"

"Keep going straight ahead for about a mile. That's where Purdon made a series of turns that muddled my sense of direction."

Paul continued along the street for twenty blocks, then slowed the car. "Do you want me to cruise around?"

"Yes, let's just play it by ear."

They found themselves in a residential neighborhood. Paul rode through a maze of sidestreets. They entered a business district and drove through a shopping mall.

"Nothing clicks so far," Eric said, disappointed.

Paul continued past the town into an unpopulated rural area. Weeds ran up to the sides of the road; the surface was rough and unpaved.

"This feels familiar," Eric said. "Follow this road."

After several miles, Alison sighed, "We're just groping in the dark, Eric."

"Exactly. Keep going. No, wait! Hold it. Do you hear that sound?"

"What sound?" Alison asked.

"It's dead ahead. A clacking-and-creaking noise. Do you see anything up the road?"

"We're as good as blindfolded ourselves, Eric. We're in a dense, overrun area without any artificial light."

"I hear it now," Alison said.

The headlights picked out the hazy outline of an irregularly shaped building.

"An old windmill!" Paul said.

The windmill was rotating slightly in a light breeze, making a rhythmic creaking noise.

Eric pulled off the handkerchief. "A windmill! I should have guessed."

"What now?" Paul asked.

"Keep going in the same direction." He asked Alison to retie the handkerchief around his eyes.

"Is this really necessary?"

"We're approaching a freight yard to our right," Paul said.

"A freight yard! That explains the train whistle I heard, and the sound of a locomotive. In about five minutes we should hit a paved road."

It was more like ten minutes. Eric was chewing his lip when Paul spotted the road. "We're entering a town named Sommersville."

"Do you see any warehouses?"

"No, the place looks pretty deserted."

"There's an old shack and an ancient firehouse," Alison said.

Paul and Alison saw it at the same instant. It loomed up suddenly out of the hazy gloom.

Eric sensed something. He felt their bodies hitch forward. "It's there, isn't it?" He ripped off his blindfold.

A solitary warehouse stood at the end of a narrow, dimly-lit street.

Eric expelled a loud breath. "That's it! Keep movin'."

"How can you be certain it's the right warehouse?" Paul asked.

"Simple. That's Fred Purdon's car over there—parked across the street!"

"Should I ride past it?"

"You'd better. Quick, the door is opening."

They parked down the block and waited as Sheriff Dolan emerged from the warehouse. He was alone. He proceeded briskly in the opposite direction and soon disappeared.

Eric turned to Paul. "From the beginning you've been urging us to call the FBI, but I was too stubborn to listen. I'm to blame for what's happened to Cindy and I'm sorry. I've also put both of you in a lot of danger. Let's find a phone booth and call them."

"What if Cindy's not in there?"

"Then we struck out. We'll just have to tell them our story."

They drove on till they came to a gas station.

"Do you want to phone?" Eric asked Paul.

"No. They're looking for you. You'd better do it."

Eric stepped into a phone booth, looked up the FBI number, and dialed.

A man answered. "Federal Bureau of Investigation."

"My name is Eric Thorne. I think I know where the kidnappers have Cindy Vaughn."

"Hold on a second. I'll transfer your call to the agents on the case."

Eric tapped his foot impatiently.

"Hello, Burke here."

Eric identified himself and explained the nature of his call.

"Where are you phoning from?"

"Sommersville."

"Is that where the child is?"

"I think she's being held in a warehouse on the corner of Barclay and Sanford."

"Barclay and Sanford? We'll find it. We'll be over as soon as possible. Wait for us."

"One more thing. Pick up Sheriff Dolan."

"Sheriff Dolan—from Millbrook?"

"He's a Nazi. We just saw him leave the warehouse."

"Well—" He sounded undecided.

"You can radio him and find out where he is. We're prepared to supply you with evidence that he's a Nazi conspirator."

"All right, we're leaving now. Where exactly will you be?"

"We'll be parked on the corner of Barclay and Ashford."

"Okay, don't do anything. Is that clear? Let us handle it." He hung up.

They drove back, parked on the corner, and settled down to wait. The street was still. An occasional car passed by. The minutes dragged. No one entered or left the warehouse.

"This waiting!" Paul said. "I wish we could get a peek inside."

"Forget it," Eric said.

Alison fidgeted in her seat. "If only they'd hurry! By this time they may have delivered Engel to the Nazis."

Twenty-five minutes had passed since Eric's call.

A blue Chevrolet cruised by. The driver parked across the street. Two men got out. They approached the car. Paul lowered the front window.

"I'm Special Agent Burke." He flashed an FBI shield. "My partner's name is Daniels."

They got into the back of the car.

Eric introduced himself and the others.

"I once took a course from your father," Burke said.

"Did you like it?" Eric asked.

"Meeting your father induced me to join the Peace Corps. It was hard for me to believe you two were really Nazis."

"We're not!" Eric said, a deep earnestness in his tone and expression.

"Has anyone else come out of the warehouse?" Burke asked.

"No."

"This is the situation. Your tip about Sheriff Dolan paid off. He confirmed that Cindy is in the warehouse, but claims that he traced his deputy and a guy named Purdon there, and went out to get reinforcements. He said he was afraid the child might be harmed if he tackled the two men alone, so he managed to convince them he was a Nazi sympathizer and wouldn't report it. According to him, they threatened to have him killed if he informed on them. The story sounds phony."

"It is phony!" Paul said hotly. "We know he's a Nazi. He attended a planning session with Eric and Werner Kleist. He pulled strings in Ivy to get the Nazis a parade permit. He's Kleist's right-hand man." Speaking rapidly, Paul explained how Eric and Alison had gotten involved with the Nazis, and related their subsequent experiences.

"We'll have to check out your story," Daniels said, "but it sounds as if you got in over your heads. I wish you had contacted us before."

Alison asked whether Engel had been turned over to the Nazis.

"It should take place in about fifteen minutes. We'll have to wait and see if Scagg and Purdon bring the child out after their confederates contact them."

"Purdon's car is parked over there," Eric said, pointing to a Ford Mustang.

"Are you sure that's his car?"

"Positive. I've ridden in that car with him."

"All right. Here's our plan. When Purdon and Scagg get the child in the car, we're going to take them."

"Are you armed?" Daniels asked.

"No," Paul and Eric said together.

"We'll have to frisk you. You, too, Alison. Sorry."

Burke and Daniels leaned over the front seat and felt for any weapons. Daniels looked inside the glove compartment. "They're clean."

"We want you to remain in this car," Burke said. "Be perfectly still. If you make a sound, it may give us away."

"Understood," Eric said.

"But what if they don't bring the child out?" Alison asked. "What if they—kill her?"

"Possibly, but not likely," Burke said. "It's a calculated risk. If we attempt to storm the warehouse, the risk to Cindy's life will be far greater."

"If they make their move," Daniels said, "it will probably come soon. Most certainly before daylight. If not, we'll proceed on an alternate plan of action."

"Okay, sit tight," Burke said. "We're going now."

They got out, ran in a low crouch, and waited in the shadows near the Mustang.

After nearly thirty minutes, the warehouse door swung open. One man came out and looked around. He went back inside, then came out with a second. Eric could not recognize either of them in the darkness, though something about them looked familiar.

186

They glanced up and down the street. It was quiet. One of them went back inside and carried out what appeared to be the body of a child.

Eric felt a cold tremor run down his back. Alison cupped a hand to her mouth.

The men walked across the street to Purdon's car and opened the door on the passenger side. They dumped the body on the back seat and stood for a moment talking.

Sitting motionless beside Paul and Alison, Eric heard Burke cry, "Freeze!" There was a brief scuffle and the sound of men's voices. Then all was quiet.

Moments passed. There was a movement at the side of the car.

Finally, Burke and his partner emerged with Scagg and Purdon in handcuffs. Daniels stood behind them with a revolver in his hand. Burke turned and leaned into the Mustang. When he stood erect, he had the child's body in his arms.

They crossed to the unmarked FBI car and pushed the two Nazis into the back seat. Daniels stood by as several other FBI men came from the nearby shadows and stood on guard at a distance surrounding the car.

Burke walked over to where the three observers waited in Mrs. Tompkins' car.

"Alison, get in the back seat, and hold Cindy." Burke waited until Alison had complied. "They gave her a sleeping pill. She's probably all right, and will be awake soon. Hold her until we get things wrapped up. And keep down in the seat—in case there's any shooting."

"Thank You, God, for protecting Cindy!" Alison

whispered. "Cindy, dear Cindy, am I glad to see you!"

"Purdon spilled the beans," Burke reported. "He denies Dolan's story. Says the abduction was Dolan's idea to begin with, that he was the one who cooked up the scheme, with Kleist's backing. Purdon and Scagg pulled the actual kidnapping, wearing rubber masks of comic-strip characters."

"Their confederates just phoned. They're on the way over with Engel. They should arrive in forty minutes."

"At the warehouse?"

"No. He's being taken to an abandoned windmill somewhere in this area. Kleist is waiting there, sharpening his teeth. We must get there before Engel does. But we're not familiar with the location and don't trust Purdon and Scagg to direct us."

A smile of relief washed over Alison's face. She exchanged glances with Eric and Paul.

"I believe we can guide you there, Mr. Burke," Eric said. "I could do it blindfolded."

# Epilogue

"We will rise again! You can't keep us down!" Kleist ranted as he was led off to one of the several FBI cars that had converged upon the area. He swung around to confront Engel, who regarded him with icy contempt. "Meddling Jew! We will wipe you and your breed off the face of the earth. We are the Master Race!"

Engel's rigid composure suddenly cracked. His hand shot forward in an accusing gesture. "Master Race? You're a tribe of vile, ignorant scavengers feeding off the humanity of decent people. You hide in the sewers and pestholes of civilization, emerging to spread your vicious gospel, then slink off to dream your foul dreams of conquest and glory."

"Our forces are regrouping throughout the United States—and the world!" Kleist shot back.

"Okay, Shicklgruber, let's go." Burke shoved the handcuffed Kleist into a car.

Engel was trembling with fury. He smashed a fist into the palm of his other hand. "How can we stamp out evil—once and for all?" His eyes turned toward the sky. "God, will the killing never stop?"

Struggling to regain his composure, Engel's eyes fell on Cindy. "Thanks to God, the child is safe."

Cindy looked at him with a sleepy smile and settled back in Alison's lap, hardly comprehending all that was being said. He patted her hand as a tear slid down his face. "I once had a little girl your age," he said hoarsely. "It was many years ago, in a different world." He turned to Alison. "The Nazis put her on a train to the Auschwitz concentration camp. She was with her mother. It was the last time I ever saw them."

Without a word, Alison took both of Engel's hands and gave them a comforting squeeze.

The FBI cars left one by one with their captured Nazi passengers.

Burke signaled Engel to get into the blue Chevrolet in which the two agents had come.

Then Burke and Daniels walked over to the car where Paul and the twins had remained, as instructed, during the FBI roundup of the Nazis. Burke leaned on the car door and slowly eyed each of the three.

"You have been of great assistance in rescuing Cindy Vaughn and capturing her abductors," he began. "Now we need your assistance in giving us detailed information about what you have discovered as the result of your personal investigation of the Phoenix operation."

"Sure. We'll be glad to fill you in, Mr. Burke," Eric offered, acting as the spokesman for the three.

"In the process of your investigations, Mr. Thorne,

190

you have risked your life. Not only that, you have allowed your sister and Paul to risk theirs—particularly in coming out here tonight."

Eric could sense a change in the agent's friendly tone. Alison began to fidget in the back seat. Cindy was becoming restless, and beginning to cry softly.

Burke paused, then continued. "I want you to think about the many implications of what you have done by taking matters into your own hands. Also we'll have to deal with such matters as failing to obey a policeman's signal and order to halt, and leaving one's home by the rear exit when police are at one's front door."

"But they did everything they did to help me build a case against the Phoenix for the attorney general," Paul explained. "I am really the one who started all this."

"Okay, okay. We won't get into that now. We'll talk about how it started and how it's ending tomorrow when we continue this cozy little chat."

Daniels opened the back door of the car and gently lifted an awakening Cindy from Alison's lap.

"Thank you, Miss, for the help with the little girl," he said to Alison.

Burke's voice became stern. "I will call at your home sometime tomorrow," he said looking at Eric. "In the meantime, you are to talk to no one—to no one—Is that clear?—about any details of this case until you receive clearance from us. That goes for all three of you. Now, go back to Ivy. Okay?"

He turned toward the FBI car where Mr. Engel was in the back seat holding Cindy, and Daniels was in the driver's seat waiting for Burke. The agent hesitated, then returned to the three in Mrs. Tompkins' car.

"I can't fault your motives for what you have done. But as private investigators, you have a lot—and I mean a lot—to learn. It's my opinion that you must have very busy guardian angels."

Burke climbed into the waiting car for the ride back to Ivy—and to Cindy's waiting parents.

The three investigators in Mrs. Tompkins' car followed.

And the windmill continued its spasmodic clicking and creaking sounds as the trio headed for Ivy's all-night car wash and gas station.